# Max

*The Ride Series, Second Generation*

## Megan O'Brien

*Max*, The Ride Series Second Generation
Copyright © Megan O'Brien 2018

Edited by Hot Tree Editing

Book design by Maureen Cutajar
www.gopublished.com

*To my fantastic readers who have loved these Knights as much as I do! I felt compelled to continue their story and so much of that drive is thanks to all of you. I hope you love this next generation just as much as the original crew!*
*XOXO*

# Prologue

The gratifying sound of the Charger's roar echoed through the garage bay as I stood up triumphantly to wipe the grease from my fingers.

"Holy shit, Wren, you actually got it runnin'?" Tatum marveled in shock.

"Course she did," my father's deep voice rumbled with pride as he sidled up alongside me to check out my handiwork.

My pop had had me working alongside him, getting our hands dirty since I was young enough to hold a wrench. I'd always been more of a tomboy, more interested in motor oil than Barbie dolls. My parents never pressured me to be anything but.

"Good job, baby," my pop praised, clapping me on the shoulder just as Cole and Axel joined us.

As vice president of the Knights Motorcycle Club, an institution that all but ran our small town of Hawthorne, Nevada, my father, Sal Armstrong, was well known and respected throughout the area. I'd been raised within the club, which had grown exponentially over the years with the second generation rising up through the ranks.

Many of us kids were close in age and had formed a tight crew. We watched each other's backs, and though many of us weren't related by blood, we were a closer family than I'd ever observed anywhere else. My family was the club—its members and their wives and children. I'd never known any different. I didn't want to.

"She got it running," Tate informed his father, Cole Jackson, one of my father's closest friends and the club prez.

Cole shot me a knowing grin, his blue eyes shining. "I'm sure she did."

"I think I'll take her for a spin. Tate, you in?" I asked with a raised brow. At eighteen, Tate and I were the same age. Though he drove me batshit crazy most of the time, he was like a brother to me.

"Hell yes," he replied emphatically, grabbing his cut and hopping into the passenger seat.

"I'll see you at home, Pop." I waved, sliding into the driver's seat and revving the engine a bit. I couldn't help myself.

He shot me a warning look, which I'd seen more times in my life than I could count. He wanted me to be careful, and I would be—relatively speaking at least. I had a bit of a lead foot, everyone knew it, but I could handle myself. They knew that too.

I was the picture of calm most of the time, with one very large exception. An exception that was pulling his Harley up to the club as we were driving away.

Max Jackson.

I'd been in love with Max for as long as I could remember. What had begun as a childhood crush had bloomed into something much more powerful over the years. At eight years my senior, Max had always treated me like one of the kids. With every passing year, his indifference, especially when I felt like my heart would explode at the mere sight of him, got harder and harder for me to bear.

I tried not to stare as he swung a muscled thigh over his bike before raking his hands through his head of thick dark hair. When his brown eyes landed on me, he watched impassively as we passed.

Tatum threw up a two-fingered salute in greeting as we made our way toward the access road that bordered the club headquarters.

"You make up your mind about school?" Tate asked as I hit the gas, trying to beat back the emotion seeing Max always incited. With us both being part of the club, that was nearly every day. It was seriously exhausting.

"No," I admitted with a sigh. I'd been accepted to a few different colleges and was still making up my mind if I wanted to move away. Part of me wanted to stay close to home while the other part felt as though it might be time to branch out.

"Not much time left," he pointed out unhelpfully.

I shot him an annoyed glance. "Yeah, I know." I envied Tatum. For him, his future was clear. He'd wanted to follow in his father's footsteps since he could walk. He'd recently patched in and felt as though his life was made.

He shrugged, undeterred by my ire. "Just sayin'. Did you think about your pop's offer?" He was referring to the fact that my dad had given me the option of working as a mechanic for the club. While I loved the idea in theory, I wasn't sure I could stomach continuing to see Max every day.

Max tended to keep to himself. He was reserved, the type that only spoke when he really had something to say. From what I could tell, he was selective when it came to women, or at least more so than many of the members. But whenever I did see him with another woman, I wanted to die and vomit at the same time.

"Jesus, Tate, you're as bad as my folks," I griped, clenching the wheel in aggravation. "I'm thinking it all over. I just need more time."

"All right, all right, don't get your panties in a twist."

"You're lucky you're pretty," I muttered, used to our standard banter.

He chuckled good-naturedly as the Charger growled, picking up speed.

\* \* \*

The house party was in full swing that Friday night as Olivia and I walked into the chaos, arm in arm. As Axel Black's daughter, Liv was also a daughter of the Knights MC and well acquainted with the life. We'd been best friends since birth.

Tonight's party had nothing to do with the club and was instead your standard high school party, complete with the expected keg and perhaps unexpected... skinny dipping? I squinted to get a better look out back. Yep, those were definitely naked girls in the pool. A bit early for that, but whatever. I grabbed Liv and myself a beer as we stood talking with some of our classmates in the kitchen. We'd been vague with our parents on our plans for the evening, otherwise risking being forced to bring one of the guys with us. There wasn't one member of the club, no matter how young, that wouldn't intimidate the hell out of this crowd, and there were times when Olivia and I just wanted to feel like your average teenager.

"Jared is totally staring at you," Olivia told me quietly, her gaze across the room. "Maybe he'll actually try to talk to you tonight since we're without a bunch of scary-ass bikers." She grinned.

I rolled my eyes, not interested in the least in Jared or any other boy my age. No, only one person would do for me, and he was all man. All confident, lethal, masculine man. Wanting Max made conjuring interest in a high school boy completely impossible. I didn't even try.

"Here he comes." She grinned around the rim of her cup, clearly amused.

"Great," I muttered dryly. Jared had been showing an interest in me for the past year but hadn't outright asked me out, which was a relief since that meant I hadn't needed to reject him.

"Hey, Wren," he greeted with an easy grin. As far as high school boys went, Jared was a handsome one, and he was in high demand if the glares I was getting from the other girls in the room said anything about it.

"Hi," I greeted, glaring at Liv as she very conveniently made herself scarce. She was the only person who knew about my feelings for Max, and tired of seeing me heartbroken over it, she was constantly pushing me toward other boys.

"Crazy we're almost done, huh?" he asked. "Have you decided where you're going to school?"

That was the question of the hour apparently.

"Not yet," I shook my head. "You?" I didn't really care, but it seemed impolite not to ask.

"Not yet," he answered vaguely.

"Ah." I nodded, trying to look interested.

"Listen," he began as I braced for whatever he was about to say. "If you're around—"

He paused as a commotion sounded by the front door. A moment later, I groaned as Tatum, along with Olivia's oldest brother, Maddox, strode in, outfitted in their standard cuts, the Knights MC logo bright and bold on their backs as they searched the room.

When he saw me, Tatum's face spread into a devilish grin. I glared at him as the other girls in the room began preening. Suddenly, there were far better options than Jared to be had. It didn't escape my notice that at the appearance of Tate and Mad, Jared didn't delay in making himself scarce.

"You suck," I hissed when they drew closer. "How did you even know we were here?"

"Max sent us." Maddox replied, his gaze sliding over the girls in the room, looking bored. "I'll go find Liv," he added, wandering off to find his sister.

"Max?" I demanded, incredulous. This wasn't the first time he'd sent the guys after us. It made no sense to me. He barely talked to me. I wasn't even sure he liked me, much less cared how I spent my time. "Why the hell does he care?"

"Probably just tryin' to stay in Sal's good graces." Tate shrugged. "Whoa, are those chicks naked?" His brows rose as he caught sight of the pool. "This party just got interesting."

"Nuh-uh." I shook my head. "If Liv and I don't get to enjoy

this party, then you don't either." I grabbed his jacket, pulling him toward the door. I suddenly had a much more important place to be.

When we arrived at the club on the back of Tate and Mad's bikes, I was steaming mad. I stomped into headquarters, scanning the crowded room until I found him. Standing by the pool table with a club cherry looking on, Max was focused on the game and, as always, infuriatingly handsome.

Feeling bold with frustration, I stole the pool cue right out of his hand. "Why?" I demanded by way of greeting.

"Um, we're in the middle of a game," the blonde whined.

I shot her a glare.

"Get lost, Kelly," he told her dismissively before his dark eyes returned to me. "Why what?" he asked, undeterred by my temper.

"Why did you send the goon squad to come get us? Did my dad make you do that?"

"No."

His response was a surprise. "Then why?" I sputtered.

For a moment, I swore I saw a flash of something in his expression, something other than the standard veil of aloofness he sported so well. "Because you two shouldn't be at a party like that without a man on you."

"Says who?"

"Says me," he growled.

My heart pounded at the passion in his tone. "Why do you care?" I whispered, fervently hoping he'd say something—anything to provide me with a glimmer of hope that after all these years maybe, just maybe, he felt something for me too.

As though a door had slammed shut, his expression turned blank as his mask slid back into place. "I don't." He shook his head and gestured for Kelly to wobble back over in her four-inch heels.

My gut twisted at his cool words as he slid an arm around the bimbo at his side. "You're an ass, Max. You know that?" I hissed, turning and stalking away.

The only silver lining, and it was really more a gray one than anything, was that he'd just made my decision easy.

I had to get the hell out of here.

# Chapter 1

The persistent gray sky and canopy of lush trees accompanied me as I pointed my car for home on a typical overcast day in Portland, Oregon. When I'd moved here for school just over three years ago, the near constant rain and dark skies had felt downright oppressive. Now, they were merely a burden I accepted, a reward of sorts for when the sun finally shone for those scant summer months.

I pulled up to the one-story bungalow Olivia and I shared. For a while, it had been an ideal situation; after all, Liv and I were like sisters and lived well together. It wasn't by accident we'd decided on the same school. Our house was walking distance to downtown and had plenty of space.

It would have been perfect with the exception of the weird packages and letters that had begun arriving for me around six months ago. At first, they had started off small, a simple poem or quote or a small bouquet of flowers. But recently the gifts had become a bit more extravagant, including jewelry and clothing. It was seriously creepy.

I shed my ever-present rain jacket and boots upon entering our living room before heading for the kitchen. After a day of back-to-back classes, I was ready to eat and sleep, in that order.

The house was quiet as I rummaged through our fridge in search of an easy dinner.

"Hey," Livie's soft voice greeted. "Hungry?" She laughed at my focused attempt to dig through the fridge.

"Aren't I always?" I replied dryly.

"True," she agreed, leaning against the doorway, watching my ministrations. "Class okay?"

I shrugged as I moved to the counter to prep a sandwich. I was too hungry to come up with anything more creative. "You know me, school isn't my favorite thing, but I'm making it through." We were in the midst of finals, and my stress level was at an all-time high.

She nodded knowingly.

"How are you? How was your day?" I wanted to know.

"Fine," she replied. "I think I did okay on that test."

No doubt she'd aced it. Unlike for me, school seemed to come naturally to Livie.

"I'm sure you did," I assured her. The silence stretched between us as I debated asking her the question I dreaded the most.

There was no need, as was typical between us, she read my mind without my having to speak. "Nothing today," she murmured quietly.

My breath of relief was short lived.

"I, um, may have mentioned the deliveries to my dad," she shared with a grimace.

I just barely saved the glass I nearly knocked off the counter in my haste to whirl around toward her. "For shit's sake, Liv, do you want them coming down here?" I demanded. We barely kept our fathers and the rest of the Knights at bay as it was. It had been hard on our overprotective families to have us so far away. The fact we were together appeased them some, that and the fact that my dad, a security specialist for the club, had rigged the security in our house to a ridiculous degree before we'd moved in. He'd said it was a requirement for me to go to school here.

"I'm sorry, Wren, but that shit is seriously skeeving me out. I think they should know about it. It's been going on a long time."

I rummaged in my bag for my phone, which I'd had on vibrate through class, and groaned at the amount of phone calls and texts I'd missed. "Dammit, Liv!" I chastised her as I saw that my dad had called three times and Tatum once. But it was the missed call and text from Max that had my heart lurching.

*What the fuck is going on? Call me back.*

Max checked in on me now and then, but for the most part, I kept him at arm's length. After the way we'd left things, I didn't understand why he checked in at all.

I curled up on the sofa with my plate of food as Liv plopped down beside me.

"You're not gonna answer him?" she pressed.

"Nope." I shook my head, taking a giant bite of my sandwich.

She sighed in aggravation but didn't press.

"We going out tomorrow?" I asked.

She made a grumbling noise at the subject change but nodded nonetheless. "Sure. Jilly's?" she suggested.

It was our favorite bar within walking distance from the house.

"Sounds good," I agreed, flipping on the television and scrolling to our latest dramedy addiction.

*        *        *

The next night, plied with much needed caffeine after a full day, I stood next to Liv as we got ready for a night out. I'd chosen my standard black jeans, a loose-fitting green sweater, and boots. Portland was perpetual sweater weather, and I'd begrudgingly embraced the look, though I missed the strappy sandals and sundresses I'd worn at home. Despite being a tomboy at heart, I'd never dressed like one. I left my long black hair down and loose around my face. With a swipe of eyeliner on my blue eyes and some gloss on my full lips, I was ready.

Livie was dressed similarly, though where my figure was tall and lean, Liv was curvy with an ass I envied on a frequent basis. She'd swept her blonde hair up into a loose bun, her only makeup a swipe of mascara on her gorgeous brown eyes.

"Ready?" she asked with a raised brow.

"Ready." I nodded.

I linked my arm through hers as our boots hit the wet pavement in a rhythmic splash that had become a soundtrack of sorts since we'd moved here.

Once we posted up at our favorite bar, we relaxed over a few drinks and some good music. It was one of those nights where nothing specular was happening, and that was part of the joy of it—special in its simplicity.

"Holy shit. Is that Jared Waters? From high school?" Liv's eyes were squinted across the dimly lit bar.

I swiveled to follow her line of sight. "Looks like it," I replied, spotting him by the entrance. "I didn't realize he went to school here."

"He probably followed you since he's so in loooove with you," she teased, making a kissy face.

I rolled my eyes. "Right. And he's coming over." I sighed. I so wasn't in the mood for small talk.

"Hey, Wren, Olivia," he greeted, looking surprised to see us. "I didn't realize you guys went to school here."

"We were just saying the same thing." I nodded, delivering what I hoped was a friendly smile. Just because I'd never returned his feelings didn't mean I should be a dick.

"I transferred in this year," he explained. "Can I get you girls a drink?" he offered with a raised brow toward the bar.

"Su—" Liv was about to agree as I cut her off abruptly.

"No, thanks. We're good." I didn't want to lead him on, and frankly, I wanted to spend the evening with Liv, not some guy from high school I barely knew.

He shrugged easily enough. "All right, well I'm sure I'll see you around. Have a good night."

"You too," I said in parting before turning back to a glaring Liv.

"What the hell, Wren?" she growled, or tried to. That was the thing about Liv, she couldn't pull off angry very well. She always just ended up looking like an adorable little bunny rabbit when she scrunched up her nose. "He's cute and nice and has always been into you. Don't you think it's time you gave another guy a shot and stopped holding out for Max?"

"I'm not holding out for Max," I protested. "I was just never interested in Jared."

She raised a brow. "Or any of the other guys who have asked you out."

I shrugged. "Or them either," I agreed.

She sighed in consternation and took a swig of her drink. I knew I drove her crazy, but at least she loved me and would ultimately support me no matter how much she might want to challenge me.

After all, that was what friends were for, right?

# *Chapter 2*

WREN

It was a particularly rainy evening when I made my way to my car after my last final three days later. Summer was upon us, but you'd never know it based on the weather. Despite the gloomy evening, I felt as though a weight had been lifted off my shoulders with finishing finals. No more studying—at least until the fall.

My boots clomped noisily on the ground as I spotted my car, one of the few left in the parking lot. I had my keys out ready to unlock it when I was slammed into from behind. The force of it sent my head crashing into the side of my car, my backpack flying off my shoulder as my knees gave out beneath me.

I sat dazed for a second before my assailant yanked me to my feet by my hair. It was then I got my first real look at him. He was a huge, bald-headed man with beady eyes and a grim smile that sent a chill racing down my spine. "Damn, you're cute. Looks like I'll have to take another type of reward," he leered.

I recoiled from him. "You're disgusting," I spat, bringing a knee up and missing my goal by a few crucial inches, hitting his upper thigh instead.

His expression darkened with fury before an even more unsettling look resembling glee had a smile ghosting across his lips. "You want to play rough, little mama? Fine, we'll play rough." He growled as he pulled my head back even farther.

His fist flew to my face, its force delivering a painful blow that nearly knocked me unconscious. He released his grip, and I staggered, trying to keep my balance.

"Just take my wallet." I panted, feeling like I might faint or pass out.

"Wren!" The vaguely familiar voice calling from across the lot sent a shot of relief through me.

My assailant grumbled to himself before hesitantly letting me go and loping off in the opposite direction.

"Wren, oh my God! Are you okay?"

I looked up through one eye, the other having swelled shut, to find Jared peering over me with concern.

"I think so." I reached out to grasp his arm for balance.

"I'm going to call the cops," he said, pulling out his phone as he wrapped an arm around me to steady me.

"Can you also call Liv? Ask her to come?" I asked in a small voice.

"Sure," he agreed gently.

The next hour was chaotic as the police arrived almost at the same time as a frantic Olivia who rushed to my side, grasping my hand in hers where it stayed the entire time I gave my statement.

Even after the police excused him, Jared stayed, saying he

wanted to make sure I was okay. Even in my foggy state of mind, I thought that was considerate of him.

"You'd never seen him before?" the police officer asked. I'd already answered that question, and after an hour of describing my ordeal, I was more than ready to be done.

I shook my head in frustration. "No. Like I said, I thought maybe he wanted to steal my wallet, but he didn't even take it. He said something about taking another type of reward, like another one had been offered to him, but I have no idea what that meant," I explained, feeling exhausted.

"Are we all done?" Olivia spoke up assertively. "We've been over all the details. I'd like to get my friend home."

The officer looked me over and nodded, slapping his notebook shut. "We'll be in touch if we have any more questions."

Liv put an arm around me, guiding me toward her car.

"I can drive you girls home," Jared offered.

She looked over her shoulder at him. "That's okay, I've got it. Thanks so much, Jared. I'm so grateful you were here."

"Me too," he replied, his gaze trained on me. "Maybe she should go get checked out. That eye looks bad."

"I'll take care of it," Liv replied firmly, obviously eager to get me out of there. She guided me into the passenger side of her car before running around to the other side.

Jared was still standing there watching us worriedly as we drove out of the lot.

"I don't need a hospital," I told her. I just wanted to get home, put some ice on my eye, and curl up in a protective ball.

"I'll take you home, and then I'll call Laurie, see what she recommends," she told me, referring to the head nurse at

Hawthorne Community Hospital and wife of Tag, who'd been a member of the Knights for as long as I'd been alive.

"Okay," I agreed as I sat with my eyes closed, pain radiating through me.

"We need to call home, Wren." Her voice was quiet but firm. "I know you've put it off, but between the weird packages at the house and now this, I think we need help."

I hadn't thought about the two things being related, but even still, the last thing I wanted was to put my friend in danger, and it was with that thought that I agreed. "I'll do it," I mumbled.

She sighed in obvious relief as we neared home, pulling to the curb. She helped me inside and onto my bed as she rushed about getting ice.

After she had me situated, she left the room to call Laurie while I lifted my phone to my ear. I didn't even think as I hit his name. Ruled by instinct and vulnerability, I just did what came as naturally as breathing.

"Wren." Max's voice washed over me when he answered, surprise clear in his tone. His voice alone had the tears I'd fought all evening filling my eyes and clogging my throat. "Wren?" he demanded, worried now.

"I..." I had to clear my throat and swallow hard to continue. "I'm okay," I managed. "But this man... he attacked me when I was walking to my car," I shared.

"What?" Max's reply was a thunderous bellow. "Where are you now?"

"Liv drove me home."

"Are you hurt?" he demanded as I heard other male voices in the background.

"I'm banged up but nothing serious. Liv is going to call Laurie." My voice wobbled as I tried to control the desire to sob openly.

He must have caught on since his tone was much softer when he spoke again. "All right, Wren, listen to me. The minute we hang up, I'm on my bike headed for you. In the meantime, there's a club we trust nearby, the Blue Devils. I'm gonna ask them to ride out to you and stay until I can get there. Wren, you get me?" he pressed when I'd remained silent.

"Okay," I agreed hoarsely.

"It's gonna be okay. I'm gonna take care of this."

I believed him. "Okay," I repeated. "Drive safe."

"See you soon." His tone was clipped as he disconnected.

I sighed in exhaustion, sitting on the edge of my bed holding my phone in my hand. I couldn't believe I'd called him. Why had I called *him*?

Olivia poked her head in, eyeing me with concern.

"Max is coming," I mumbled.

To her credit, she didn't even look surprised. "Sounds about right," she agreed instead.

Whatever the hell that meant.

# Chapter 3

## WREN

True to Max's word, the Blue Devils had arrived within what felt like minutes after I'd hung up with him. Three hulking men in leather vests now took up residence in our small home. They'd instructed us to hole up in my room, which was where we could be found hours later, cuddled on my bed together.

Laurie had helped Liv to confirm I didn't have a concussion and didn't require a hospital visit. Instead, she suggested pain killers and ice to relieve the swelling.

I had just fallen into a deep sleep, after a night of startling awake anytime I dozed off, when a commanding knock sounded on my bedroom door.

It swung open, and a hulking figure blocked the light from the hallway.

It had been years since I'd set eyes on Max, having expertly avoided him in my visits back home. I wasn't surprised that I was no less affected by him. If anything, the strength of my reaction had increased with time and distance.

The sheer power and masculinity he excluded was eclipsed only by the beauty of his face as he stared at me with unapologetic intensity. His dark eyes assessed me intently.

"Wren."

My name had never sounded so beautiful than when spoken with his deep, gravelly voice.

"You okay, sweetheart?" he demanded gently as he crouched beside the bed, his size dwarfing everything around him.

"Never better," I replied with a forced smile as I sat up with a slight wince. I was suddenly very aware that I was only dressed in a thin tank top as his gaze roved my frame as though assuring himself I was whole.

His gaze softened at my attempt at levity. "Somehow, I doubt that." A sad smile quirked the edges of his full lips. "You girls get dressed," he directed, rising back to his full height. "Come out when you're done." With that gentle command, he strode from the room.

"Damn, he's intense," Livie muttered. "He didn't even look at me, by the way," she pointed out, not sounding perturbed in the least.

I ignored her comment as I stood up, rifling through my clothes and pulling out a pair of jeans and my coziest sweater. Liv slipped down the hall to get dressed herself before we both headed out to the living room where Gunner stood talking to Max. Best friends since grade school, where one man went, the other was usually close behind. He stood shoulder to shoulder with Max, his hair shaved close to his skull, black and gray tattoos decorating both arms, and wearing the ever-present Knights cut.

"Hey, Gunner," Livie greeted softly.

He turned a worried gaze to both of us, his formidable countenance softening. "Hey, Livie. Wren, damn." He winced when he got a look at me.

I simply stared at the five huge men in our living room, completely overwhelmed and exhausted. It all felt surreal, like someone else's nightmare—well, if I hadn't been attacked, maybe it would be a fantasy given the amount of male beauty that was currently filling my living room.

"Do you need anything?" Olivia asked the unfamiliar bikers. "Sorry we didn't offer...." She trailed off, ever the hostess.

"No, girl," one of the Blue Devils grunted. We hadn't bothered with introductions.

Max spoke to both of us, though his gaze was locked on me. "I need you to pack any shit you need over the next few days, gotta be small enough to fit in a backpack since we're takin the bike. We're bringing you home," he stated. "Both of you," he added, his gaze swinging from me to Liv.

I counted to five in my head, trying to control my reaction. "I am not coming home with you, Max. I have a job lined up for the summer, and why does Liv have to go too? That makes no sense!" I protested.

"Christ." Max looked to the ceiling, as though searching for patience before his eyes met mine. "You've been getting packages for months now, which by the way we're gonna have words as to why the fuck you kept that from us." He glowered. "Some sick fuck is probably stalking you. And now you get attacked? We're not leaving you or Liv here unprotected. So, I'm going to tell you again. *You* are comin' home with *me*."

The idea of being on the back of his bike had my insides liquefying despite his surliness.

I eyed him intently, cocking my head. "People still always do what you say?"

He stared back at me. "The smart ones do."

"Maybe your measure of intelligence is skewed," I replied dryly.

His lips quirked into a semblance of a smile. "Glad to see you haven't lost that quick wit."

Despite his compliment causing my belly to flip, I wasn't done. I'd never been one to take orders from anyone, not even a hot-as-hell, occasionally scary Max Jackson. "The cops have my statement. Maybe they'll catch the guy," I put in, knowing I was grasping at this point.

His nostrils flared. "Cops can chase their tails all they want. We'll do our own brand of hunting." There was a dark intent to his words that I didn't want to explore just then. "We're dealing with this, our way. I know it means leaving your life here, but if it means you get to keep livin' that life, well then, you're just gonna have to be okay with that."

I stared at him, stunned into rare silence.

"It also means you get to see the fucking sun once in a while," Gunner muttered.

He had a point there.

"Okay," I agreed quietly. What else could I really say?

Max nodded. "Okay. Both of you get the shit you need for the next day or so. We've got prospects in route to box up the rest. One of us will deal with your landlord."

My head was spinning as the Knights MC effectively took over my life, *again*.

"Liv, you're with Gun. I'll take Wren."

The thought of being pressed against him for hours on end was both daunting and thrilling as my scrambled brain attempted to process everything that had happened in the last twenty-four hours.

As though reading my mind, Liv took my hand, leading me back to my room. She seemed completely steady while I felt like I was completely unraveling.

I looked at her, meeting the quiet determination in her eyes. She didn't want this either, but she was accepting it. I was suddenly determined to do the same.

"I'm sorry, Liv," I murmured regretfully.

She offered a small smile. "You know what? It's okay. We're done with school for the summer, and I was already on the fence about what to do. I don't mind going home for a while, especially if you'll be there."

"You're such a good friend. I don't deserve you." I sighed as she busied herself helping me pack up. "Make sure you pack my anti-frizz serum, you know how this hair situation can get." I gestured to my mass of black waves.

"First thing I packed." She winked with a grin.

It was with that simple, seemingly trivial detail between friends in the midst of a nightmare that had me returning her smile.

# Chapter 4

Four hours later, my ass and thighs were numb after years of not being on a bike as Max pulled off the highway.

"What are we doing?" I asked in confusion when we pulled into a motel parking lot and he cut the engine.

"You need a break from the bike," he stated swinging off the bike.

I remained seated, my stubborn streak roaring to life. I didn't want to slow us down. "I'm fine. I can keep going."

"Yeah, maybe you can," he allowed. "But I can't." It was then that I noticed the circles under his eyes, the five o' clock shadow at his jaw. "I need to catch a few hours of sleep. Going on almost a day without any," he explained. "Not gonna risk it. Especially not when you're on the back of my bike." He shook his head. "We'll meet Liv and Gunner in Hawthorne."

A lot of men I'd known would never admit they were tired; they'd see it as a sign of weakness. But that had never been Max. Everything he did, he owned with a confidence he'd exuded since he was a kid. If possible, it made him even more attractive.

He unclipped his helmet, quirking a brow at me. "You gonna get off the bike sometime today?"

I wrinkled my nose. "I'm afraid that if I do, my torso will move independently from the rest of my body. I think my ass might be permanently imprinted on the seat."

He barked out a laugh as he reached under my chin to unclip my helmet. "Come on, I'll help you." His large hand completely dwarfed mine as he gently guided me off the bike. "Those muscles have a short memory. It's been a few years, huh?"

I nodded begrudgingly as I stood up, awkwardly trying not to look like a bow-legged geek.

"I just need to catch a couple of hours, and we'll get back on the road," he explained as he strode toward the front office. "I want to make it back to Hawthorne by late afternoon."

We'd left Portland at dawn. It was now just after breakfast time, but I felt like I could definitely use a few hours of sleep myself after a restless night.

When he booked one room with two beds, I tried to muffle my squeak of surprise.

Unsurprisingly, he still caught it. Nothing had ever gotten passed him. "Not gonna be using the room long," he stated simply.

"Fine. As long as there's a bathtub," I mumbled. My numb extremities definitely needed a solid soak.

Max raised an inquiring brow toward the motel manager.

"There's a tub," the man answered quickly, seeming nervous in Max's presence.

I couldn't say I blamed him.

"Fuckin great," Max replied, taking the key the manager handed him.

"Do you scare people on purpose or is it just a Max Jackson side effect?" I asked as we ascended the stairs to our room.

"Max Jackson side effect?" He chortled. "What exactly would those side effects be?"

I had a whole set of personal side effects, but that wasn't what we were talking about. "Aside from scaring the general population? Including unsuspecting motel managers?" I quipped as he let us into the room and deposited my backpack on the bed farthest from the door.

"Yeah, aside from that." His mouth was doing that delicious quirking thing again.

"I can't say at the moment, still gathering all the intel."

He grinned. "Let me know what you come up with. Now, are you gonna stop with the sass so I can get some sleep?"

"I'll try." It was the best I could do.

He moved toward the bathroom, shaking his head at me. When he re-emerged, he was stripping off his cut, the muscles in his arms rippling deliciously with the movement.

At thirty, Max was more gorgeous than he'd ever been. He'd added more tattoos to the beautiful landscape that was his body. He'd gotten bigger, more muscular, but it was his eyes that had always done me in, and still did. Warm chocolate brown, like melted chocolate framed by dark lashes. He was truly breathtaking, as was evidenced by my loss of breath.

He stepped closer toward me, stopping slightly to peer at my face. "Did you ice your face when it happened?"

"I did," I replied quietly. "Didn't help much though." I grimaced. The bruise around my temple was nearly black and still sore to the touch.

"Might have helped more than you think," he replied. "Sorry as hell it happened though." His wretched expression conveyed just how true that was.

"Me too," I agreed, trying not to get caught up in the tenderness he was exhibiting. "I'll let you get some sleep," I continued, stepping away from him. "I'll take a bath and try to reinject some feeling into my body."

He chuckled, the sound low and rich.

While the warm water helped my sore body, it did nothing to soothe my frazzled nerves. The minute I lay back against the cool tile and closed my eyes, all I could picture was the man's look of glee as he hit me, and the sound of my flesh being pounded into.

A soft knock rapped against the door. "Wren? You all right?"

I sat up straighter, water sloshing around me. "Fine," I called, my voice coming out far too high pitched.

"You sure?" he sounded skeptical.

"Yeah. I'll be out in a second," I replied, mortified that I must have made some sort of noise that concerned him. I rose up out of the tub, drying off hastily and throwing my clothes back on.

When I emerged, a cloud of steam around me, Max was on his back on top of the covers, his arm thrown behind his head. His eyes tracked my movements as I lay down on the unoccupied bed. "Sorry," I murmured, my face flushed both from embarrassment and the hot bath.

His head turned on the pillow, and I felt his penetrating gaze as I stared up at the ceiling. "What's getting to you?" he asked quietly.

"I'm fine."

"You're not, but you might be if you get it out. It'll eat at you otherwise."

I wondered if he was speaking from personal experience.

"You need to sleep," I argued.

"No offense, sweetheart, but I'm not gonna be able to sleep with all those whimpering noises you keep making."

I turned my head, regarding him in horror. "I was making whimpering noises?"

He eyed me steadily. "Nothing to be ashamed of. I wouldn't want to live in a world where what happened was something you took lightly."

The silence that followed was surprisingly comfortable as I rolled to my side to face him. He watched me expectantly. There was something about his steadiness, his confidence, that settled me.

"I keep seeing his face. I'm afraid it'll haunt me."

"It won't." He sounded so sure.

I narrowed my eyes at him. "How can you be so sure?"

"Because he won't be breathing for long," he replied without hesitation. "And he'll never hurt you again. Nothing will." The conviction in his tone had me wondering if maybe there was a small possibility he felt something for me.

"My experience? Inner demons are what really haunt you," he continued. "Shit you haven't dealt with, things you regret, things that brought out the worst in you. People you love who've let you down. Something like this? It's fear and some pain, but it's not a demon you can't shake, not unless you let it be."

"You know something about this," I deduced, holding his gaze. It was the most we'd spoken in years, and despite the subject, I relished the sound of his voice, of getting just a piece of him, no matter how small.

He turned his head, pondering the ceiling. "Yeah." His reply left no room for further conversation.

"Thanks, Max," I murmured quietly.

I couldn't help but want to slay some of those demons Max seemed to be fighting. Somehow, I knew the battle scars just might be worth it.

# Chapter 5

MAX

Like a fucking creep, I watched her sleep. I couldn't seem to help it. It was taking everything in me not to head back to her place in Portland and lie in wait for anyone who even thought about hurting her. The fact she'd been attacked, that I'd been so far away when it happened, didn't sit well with me.

I'd always been protective of Wren. She wasn't like the other girls. She was something special, always had been.

Not many women knew their way around a motor the way she did. She was tough, unafraid to get dirty or speak her mind. She was also sweet and looked soft as hell. She was a fiery ball of contradiction that I longed to unravel.

And now, now I felt that same protectiveness, except it was something... more. Something that struck deep the second I saw her. For years I hadn't seen her as anything other than a kid, but she'd always been pretty. But, Christ, she'd turned into a beautiful woman. Those huge blue eyes that looked so damn determined, that mass of dark hair my fingers itched to be buried in, and those bee-stung lips that I wanted to bite first and kiss second.

But she was too young for me, and she was Sal's daughter, his *only* daughter for fuck's sake. As our VP, Sal didn't take any shit, and he was like an uncle to me. He'd never forgive me if I went there, and he might not be the only one. I couldn't lose my club. It was my life. My family. So, I wouldn't. I'd keep my distance, like I had ever since she'd grown a pair of tits and my cock had stood up and taken notice.

I reached down and adjusted myself at the mere memory of her in that little red bikini one summer at the lake. I'd had to turn my bike around and leave, not able to bear the sight of her lush skin and that smile I swore, when pointed at me, lit up my world in a way I'd never known before or after her.

Distance. Right.

I'd get her back to Hawthorne and make myself scarce. I could do that. There just wasn't another option.

# Chapter 6

We rode into Hawthorne just as the sun was sliding beneath the horizon. Ever since we'd woken up at the motel after a few hours of sleep, Max had reverted back to the removed, surly personality I was used to. Aside from making sure I was okay to get back on the bike, he'd barely said a word. Clearly, our heart-to-heart earlier had been a fluke. I tried not to be completely dejected by that.

When we pulled up to my parents' house, I was unsurprised to find them both waiting on the porch, my pop's arm firmly around my mom's shoulders. Worry shone clear on my mom's face while my dad was biting back obvious fury.

Max cut the engine, turning to help me off the bike as my mom rushed to me, wrapping me in a hug so tight she had me grunting on impact.

"Easy, Birdie," my dad chided, using the nickname he'd called my mom for as long as I could remember. He slid an arm around both of us. "Christ, your face." He glowered once he got a look at me.

"I'm okay," I tried to reassure them both as I pulled out of their embrace. As their only child, I was used to both of them being a bit overly zealous when it came to me. I was sure this situation was about to push them into overdrive.

"Take her inside, baby," my dad asked my mom as he turned his eyes to Max. "A word," he growled.

Max nodded as I watched him over my shoulder, my mom guiding me inside. I didn't know when I'd see him again. The realization caused that ever-present ache, the one I'd left Hawthorne to unsuccessfully eradicate, to resurface with a painful blow.

His dark eyes lifted to mine once, and I swore I saw feeling there, something he tried to hide before he looked away.

I bit back tears that my mom likely thought were from everything that happened and let her guide me into the house.

\*   \*   \*

"I'm going to kill my parents," I groaned to Liv two days later as I sat on her bed. "I feel like I'm in prison. They're never going to let me go back to Portland, not that I really want to," I admitted. "Do you think you'll go back?"

She shrugged. "Maybe. The thought of going back without you feels weird though. Have you seen he-who-shall-not-be-named?" she asked cautiously.

I shook my head. "No, I'm sure he's back in indifference mode now that we're home safe."

She eyed me thoughtfully. "In the past, I've agreed. He's always been aloof with you. But I don't know, this time it seemed different to me. The way he looked at you, there was something there, Wren."

I groaned. "Don't put ideas in my head. The last thing I need is to get any sort of hope when it comes to Max."

She shrugged. "Just sayin', babe. The man had eyes for you. Whether he wants to ever admit that or not is a different story."

"You girls want some brownies? Fresh out of the oven!" Liv's mom, Sophie, called cheerfully. I was thankful for the interruption, even if my stomach would pay for it later.

Every now and then, her mom would get a wild hair to take up cooking again. It always ended up with lots of experiments gone wrong, creative discarding of whatever she'd made, and the occasional kitchen fire.

"My dog wouldn't eat the last batch," Liv warned in a low voice.

I laughed. "I think the potted plant in your living room still has some of the cookies I hid there the other day."

But the truth was, we'd always pretend. They didn't come sweeter than Liv's mom, except for maybe mine, and we'd never dream of hurting her feelings.

"Look out, Liv, your mom's cooking." Axel ducked into the room to warn us.

With his formidable frame, bushy beard, and surly demeanor to most who encountered him, Axel was an intimidating man. Fortunately, I'd never faced an angry Axel Black. I knew him as the doting husband and father he preferred to be.

"Got it, Dad. I'll get the Pepto-Bismol," Liv stated in complete seriousness.

He chuckled. "Good call, sweetheart."

The rumble of my dad's Charger sounded as we were finishing up with the brownies Sophie had made—or rather, finished hiding the brownies she'd made.

"Here's my chaperone," I grumbled to no one in particular as I gathered my jacket.

"Go easy on your pop," Axel instructed. I hadn't realized I'd spoken loud enough for him to hear. "It would be hard as hell for any father to know his daughter was beaten, to see the evidence of it on her face, and to know he couldn't stop it." He squeezed my shoulder briefly. "But I'd imagine it's harder still for a man like Sal. He just wants to protect you."

I met his gaze, resolving to bite my tongue and be more patient. "I know. You're right."

He nodded once before striding toward the kitchen as I waved my goodbyes and ran out to my dad's car.

The Charger had been the first car we'd ever worked on together. It's heady rumble and black-on-black design was one of my earliest memories.

"Hey, Pop," I greeted, sliding into the passenger seat.

His eyes swept my face a moment before he turned his eyes to the road. "Have fun?"

"Sure." I shrugged. "Sophie packed you some brownies." I held up the bag, muffling a grin.

"Fucking great." He groaned as he hit the gas. "She's runnin' a little rough," he noted, referring to the car. "Want to take a look with me when we get home?"

Despite his overprotective nature, I'd never turn down a chance to spend time with him. I grinned. "Sure thing."

# Chapter 7

WREN

The familiar smell of gasoline and rubber filled my lungs as I worked underneath my Mustang in the garage bay at the club the next day. My dad had kept her stored here for me while I was away at school, and I was anxious to get her running again.

"Shit!" I exclaimed harshly when I lost my grip on the wrench and smashed my thumb. I rolled out from underneath the car to squeeze it tight against my chest, waiting for the throbbing to stop.

"You okay?" Max's gruff voice took me by surprise. We hadn't spoken since he'd brought me back.

"What do you care?" I shot back, the pain in my thumb triggering my temper.

His brows lifted in surprise as he stood, feet braced apart, arms crossed over his broad chest. "What the fuck are you talking about?"

"Max, you act like I have the plague every time I get within a hundred feet of you," I snapped. "I don't know what in the hell I did. You didn't used to hate me so much. But it makes me feel like shit. So, by all means, don't pretend like you're concerned. Feel free to run in the other direction like you always do."

For a moment, we just stared at each other, the tension crackling like a live wire between us. I hadn't planned on being so honest. Hell, I hadn't planned on ever saying those things to him at all. But now that I had, it felt good, like a weight had been lifted off my chest. I wasn't going to apologize or back down, not now.

"You think I hate you?" His voice was an incredulous rasp.

"Maybe not hate," I allowed. "But you clearly don't like me very much. We used to actually talk to each other."

In fact, despite our age difference, years before, I'd felt like he'd actually understood me in a way that most people didn't. That all felt like a lifetime ago.

"I remember," he acknowledged quietly.

"Then what? Did I do something?"

He held my gaze, and I felt like I was drowning in the amount of intensity pooling from those dark depths. "No."

I tried desperately to hide the pain his one-word answer incited. When it was clear that was all I was going to get, I released a sad sigh. "Okay, Max." I lay back down on my roller and slid back under the car, effectively ending the conversation.

I let out a shriek when I was grabbed by the ankles and pulled back out. I stared up at him in shock as he leaned over me, fire lighting his gaze.

"There's nothing wrong with you, got it?" he demanded, our faces inches apart. "You're perfect. Don't ever think otherwise."

His gaze dropped to my lips, and for a heart-stopping moment, I thought he might kiss me. My heart pounded in my chest as my breathing accelerated. I'd never wanted anything more in my life. Then he pulled back, rising to his feet, his chest heaving. "Be careful with the wrench," he ordered brusquely before turning and striding away. The slam of the inner garage door registered his exit as I fought for breath.

*What the hell just happened?*

# Chapter 8

S*hit.*

That had been too close. Way too fucking close. But the pain in her eyes, pain I'd caused, was too much to bear. I'd had to set her straight. Having her that close had been nearly excruciating. Her full, rosy lips taunted me, her sweet smell drawing me in. I deserved a fucking medal for my restraint.

I slammed my way back in to the club, growling at any one who dared look in my direction.

"Max. My office," Cole's command had me inwardly groaning.

Fucking great.

I followed him into his office, sitting in the chair opposite his desk. "I'm talking to you as your brother right now, not as your prez," he began, sitting on the edge of his desk, looking down at me with concern. "What the hell is going on with you lately?" he demanded. "You've been in your own head more than usual and meaner than a fucking grizzly."

I clenched my jaw but remained silent.

"You're avoiding everyone, including Pop and your mom. They're worried."

Though not related by blood, Cole and I shared a father in Cal, who'd adopted me when I was seven. Despite being over twenty years my senior, Cole and I had always had a solid bond. He accepted my reserved personality, my tendency to be a loner. Except for right now apparently.

"I'm fine," I ground out.

He made a noise of frustration. "You're not. You can talk to me, Max. You know that."

Not about this. Not about Wren.

"There's nothing to talk about."

His blue eyes shone with frustration. "Fine. You don't want to talk to me? I'm not going to force you, but you need to rein your shit in. I still need you on the Rossi business tonight, but not if you're going to go off half-cocked. You get me?"

I took a deep breath in. The club had some issues with the mob wanting to expand outside of Vegas, way outside, too close to Hawthorne. That shit was not happening. "I get you. Gun and I are riding out tonight."

"Be careful." I could tell he wanted to say more, while at the same time knowing he wouldn't get more out of me.

"I will," I agreed, rising to stand and heading for the door.

"Max." His voice stopped me short. "That offer to talk? It stands, always."

I nodded once and walked through the door.

∗　∗　∗

My fist met flesh again and again, the rhythmic sound soothing in some twisted way as I took out my aggravation, my angst, on the man slumped in a chair in front of me.

Thanks to Maddox's source, we'd intercepted the member of the Rossi family with a truckload of firearms headed directly through Hawthorne.

"Max, man, enough." Gunner grunted, pulling me back.

"It's not," I ground out, the primal growl of my voice barely registering as mine.

"It is," he insisted, pushing me by the chest toward the far wall.

"Stay the fuck out of Hawthorne," I warned over my shoulder.

"Doubt he heard you, brother." Xander chortled. "He's out cold. But he heard you the other ten times you said it. I'd consider your message delivered."

"Let's go, man," Gunner coaxed, guiding me from the warehouse. "What the fuck is up with you?" he demanded, echoing Cole's earlier line of questioning. "Not saying you don't usually hold your own, but I've never seen you like that." His gaze was cautious and a little amazed as he regarded me.

Had I really gone that overboard? My bloody knuckles, so torn up you could see bone, said maybe.

"Whatever it is, you know I have your back, right?" he demanded. "Whatever it is. *Whoever* it is," he emphasized.

Fuck, he knew.

We'd been thick as thieves since grammar school. We'd patched in together. I trusted Gunner more than anyone, and he knew me better than most. That didn't mean I wanted to talk about it.

"How long has it been?" he asked quietly.

"Since what?" I ground out.

"Since you fell in love with Wren," he replied simply. He was going to force my hand. Hell, maybe it would help.

I sighed, raking a hand through my hair. "I'm not sure," I answered honestly. "A few years maybe."

"Shit, man," he muttered. "Sal's gonna kill you."

"Not if he doesn't find out," I shot back.

Gunner leaned against his bike, crossing his feet at the ankle. "Hate to say it, but there's no way you can hide it forever. I figured it out easily enough. It's all over your face when she's around. If he cares enough to pay attention, he'll notice. And you, fuck, dude, you're wound so tight you're going to fucking snap. Something has to give."

"I'll rein it in."

He chuckled. "Sure you will. About as much as she will."

My head snapped to his in surprise.

"What?" he demanded with a grin. "You're telling me you don't see the way she looks at you? You two are ridiculous." He shook his head.

The fact that Wren might feel the way I did made something foreign, but not all together unpleasant, expand in my chest. I'd never considered the possibility and instead had focused on controlling my own feelings.

"Sal will kill me," I repeated.

"Yeah, he will," Gunner agreed. "But he might also surprise you." He shrugged.

He might. But could I take that chance?

"Are we done with our little heart-to-heart?" I demanded, swinging a leg over my bike.

He chuckled. "It was beautiful, man, but yeah, sure." Gunner loved to fuck with me, always had. It was part of why we were such a good team. I kept him grounded, and he got me to lighten up every now and then.

"Fuck you," I threw back without malice as our bikes roared to life.

He merely chuckled and shot me his middle finger.

We hit the highway, my thoughts jumbled, heart pounding with the knowledge that the girl I loved might actually love me back. I knew that with that possibility, even without acting on it, my life would never be the same.

# Chapter 9

When Friday night rolled around, I was fully prepared to put my pajamas on and watch a movie with my mom. Ever since the encounter with Max, I'd been avoiding anything having to do with the club, and that included Gunner's party I'd heard was happening tonight.

When a knock sounded on my front door, I was surprised to find Livie on the other side.

"Did I forget plans we made?" I asked in confusion.

She grinned mischievously. "In a way, maybe. You're coming to Gunner's party with me. Let's go get you dressed," she directed. "Hi, Kat." She grinned at my mom as I sputtered behind her. Gunner's was the last place I wanted to go since Max was almost guaranteed to be there.

"You girls have fun." My mom smiled, turning back to her magazine.

I looked at her in wide-eyed bafflement. Of course, the one time I wanted her to lock me in my room, she was pushing me out the door.

"You could use some fresh air, Wren. You've been cooped up here with us. Wouldn't hurt to get a little dressed up, and to shower." She wrinkled her nose a bit.

"I've showered," I protested.

"Not today," she replied, as my dad sauntered into the room, dropping to her side on the couch and putting his arm around her.

"Wren and Livie are going out for a bit," she informed him with an intimate smile.

Oh gross, now I knew at least part of the reason they were so eager to get rid of me.

"Mine too," Olivia grumbled with an eye roll as she pulled me toward my room.

"I have no idea what to wear," I admitted, eyeing the cute sundress Olivia wore.

"Let me help." She moved toward my closet before I could argue otherwise. She pulled out one of my more formfitting V-neck T-shirts, my jean shorts, and booties. "I'd try to talk you into wearing something more revealing, but I know you won't go for it." She sighed dramatically.

"Thanks," I murmured, taking the clothes.

"No big." She shrugged. "I'll get you wearing stuff to show off that rack eventually." She grinned.

I rolled my eyes. "Not likely."

"Challenge accepted," she replied resolutely. "In the meantime, at least you can flaunt those stems of yours. Now go get dressed!"

"I don't know about this," I admitted, looking down at the clothes in my hand.

"Wren, what's the other option? Avoid him forever? Because

that's what you're doing, isn't it? These people are your friends, your family. The sooner you face the music, so to speak, the better off you'll be. And you're going to do it looking hot as hell, so go get dressed." She gave me a little shove, and I argued no further, doing as she said. She was right, after all.

Thirty minutes later, as we walked together up to Gunner's door, I was still pulling at my shirt.

"You look gorgeous, quit it," Liv ordered as we walked inside the single-story home, packed to the gills with a raucous crowd.

I took her hand and led her straight to the keg, pouring us both a cup. I chugged the first and immediately poured a second.

"Whoa, Wren, take it easy. You're sort of a lightweight," she reminded me worriedly.

I shrugged. "Fuck it."

She looked like she wanted to say more just as a beautiful redhead came hurdling at us, wrapping us both up in an embrace.

Though several years older than Olivia and me, Grace Jackson was like a big sister to those of us who were several years her junior. We'd idolized her when we were little. She never minded, and instead of giving us a hard time when we'd chased her around with stars in our eyes, she'd looked out for us.

She'd been the first to give me any type of advice about boys, and lord help you if you asked for fashion advice. You'd never get rid of her. Grace had always been confident, and despite her beauty, down to earth with the warmest heart I'd ever known. As Cole's oldest daughter and Cal's first grandchild, she was the princess of the Knight's MC. With gorgeous straw-berry blonde locks and startling green eyes, she was impossibly gorgeous.

Once Grace released me, I noticed that Emmie, Max's younger sister, stood with her. Emmie was much more reserved than Grace, more like her big brother, but no less thoughtful. The two of them were much like Olivia and me, best friends since childhood and still as close as ever.

"You two look hot." Gracie beamed, looking me up and down. "Liv?"

I laughed, knowing it was that obvious I hadn't dressed myself. "Yep."

Grace slipped Liv a high five. "Well, I'm glad you two were able to fly the coop for the night. The guys lightening up a bit?"

"A bit. We're here. Though I think it's just so our parents could do it." Olivia wrinkled her nose.

Grace laughed. "Well, whatever gets you here, I guess. Mine are no better. Trust me. But at least I'm not living at home."

"Don't remind us," I put in dryly, finishing the last of my beer.

"Oh look, the youngins are here," Gunner teased, coming over and tousling my head.

"Or you're just old," I replied with saccharine sweetness. Gunner and Max were the oldest of the younger Knights generation and loved to remind us of that fact, or Gunner did anyway. "I'm getting more beer." I held up my cup.

"Wren," Liv called after me worriedly, but I ignored her.

I'd just finished filling up when I spotted him off in the corner with a brunette cherry hanging on his side. It was the worst kind of déjà vu. My heart dropped to my stomach as I fought for composure. The mere sight of another woman with her hands on him was almost too much. The thought of what they'd likely be doing later definitely was.

This was why I'd left in the first place. Three years later, and it was no easier; if anything, it was harder.

When his eyes met mine, they were glassy as though he'd already had a lot to drink or hadn't slept. Maybe both. For a minute, we just stared at each other across the crowded room until the brunette leaned in and kissed his neck.

I turned away then, nearly spilling my beer in my haste to escape the sight. I made my way to the kitchen in search of something stronger than beer. When a newer prospect, whose name I couldn't remember, started plying me with shots, I accepted gratefully.

A strong buzz began to take over, and I welcomed the feeling. But it wasn't enough, not yet. I wanted to be numb.

"Stop giving her drinks," Max ordered harshly, knocking the shot I was just about to down out of my hand.

"Hey!" I protested, knowing I wobbled slightly as I turned to face him.

"I'm taking you home."

He was always so mad at me. Why was he always so mad at me?

"Don't bother," I scoffed, trying to reach for my beer before he moved it out of reach.

Olivia joined us then, followed by Gunner. "Shit, Wren, I've been looking for you."

"Here I am," I responded, theatrically sweeping my arms out at my sides.

"Shit," she groaned. "I can't take you home like this."

"I'll sober her up," Max put in.

"I'm just buzzed. I'm fine," I protested. "And I'm not a baby. And I'm definitely not *your* baby, so you can just leave me the hell alone."

"You two are like fucking dynamite," Gunner grumbled.

I looked at him in confusion as Max let out a low growl. "You. Shut up." He pointed at Gunner. "And you—" He turned to glower at me. "—are coming with me. Either up over my shoulder or you can walk out of here on your own. You choose."

If he put me over his shoulder, I might barf all over him; though I was so mad at him, the thought wasn't entirely unappealing.

"Fine. But only because I actually like your jacket and don't want to barf on it," I huffed.

He looked to be fighting a smile as he guided me in front of him through the party and straight out the front door.

The fresh air immediately lightened my buzz as he led me toward the sidewalk.

"I'd put you on my bike, but not when you're drunk, so let's take a walk." It was more of an order than a suggestion.

"I'm not drunk," I argued, and it was mostly true. "What about your date?" I demanded.

"She's not my date." He held my elbow as I tripped over an uneven patch of sidewalk.

"She kissed your neck," I accused, knowing I was giving away much more than I'd intended and not able to stop myself.

"And you didn't like that?"

"It doesn't matter what I think," I grumbled in frustration.

"It does to me." His response had me stopping short. I stared at him, his expression raging with conflict.

"Why?" I dared to ask.

He stared wordlessly at me with that unreadable expression I hated so goddamned much.

I let out a bitter laugh. "God! Why do I even bother asking? Why are you even out here with me anyway, Max? To torture me some more? Just go back to the party. I'll walk it off. I'm fine." I started walking again, only making it a few strides before I was gripped by the arm and spun around.

"Why would I torture you? What do you mean?"

I threw up my hands, letting the tidal wave of emotion I'd held back for so long rip free. "Because watching you with another woman makes me want to die. Is that what you want to hear? It makes me want to rip my own heart out and stomp on it since that would be less painful."

Before I could utter another word, his mouth was on me. His lips took mine in a commanding caress that had my heart hammering and wetness pooling between my legs. He didn't just take. He claimed. When his tongue met mine, my entire body hummed in response, wanting more, wanting everything. His large hands slid down my spine, cupping my backside with a throaty groan as he pulled me closer.

I wrapped my arms around his shoulders, relishing the feel of his firm body against mine. His hands moved up into my hair, pulling slightly as his teeth nipped at my lower lip. Kissing him was everything I'd imagined it would be. No, it was more.

Suddenly he broke away, as though I was made of fire.

"Fuck, that was a bad idea, Wren," he rasped. "We need to forget it ever happened."

Euphoria turned to a living hell, one I was used to when it came to Max. I touched my kiss-swollen lips. "I don't want that. I don't want to forget," I protested quietly.

He groaned. "We can't, Wren. I'm older than you. I'm supposed to be trying to protect you, not tryin' to get in your pants. Your father would never understand. We just... can't."

I faced him, anger mixing with hurt running through my veins. "I'm not going to beg you, Max. But I will say that, yeah, you're older than me. That mattered when we were kids. It shouldn't matter now. And my father? He'd probably be pissed, but he loves me and wants me to be happy. He'd get over it. This is less about him and more about you," I challenged. "If you don't see me as worth fighting for, then you're right, this was a mistake. Because to me, you'd be worth it all and then some."

He looked at me, conflict raging in his eyes.

I swallowed back the tears threatening to clog my throat and gave him a sad smile. "Well, I should thank you, then. Because you confirming I wouldn't be worth it? You just gave me the only real reason for me to get over you."

And with that, I strode away from him, back toward the party.

"Wren..."

I didn't turn at the sound of his voice. I couldn't. I'd loved Max for so long—most of my life. It was finally time to begin to move on. And maybe, just maybe, be free.

# Chapter 10

## MAX

When I pulled up in front of the two-story home I'd lived in since the age of seven, when Jill and Cal had brought Emmie and me home and become our parents, I inwardly groaned at the sight of Ma waiting out front.

Jill was my aunt by blood, but had been my mother for all intents and purposes for as long as I could remember.

I'd missed the last two Sunday breakfasts. With the text from my pop this morning demanding my presence, I knew I either needed to show up or risk him knocking at my door. He would too. I'd never doubt it.

"Hi, Ma," I greeted as I strode to the front door, helmet in hand.

She wrapped me in a hug, pulling back to look into my eyes. "You're not sleeping," she deduced correctly.

"I'm all right," I assured her.

She bit her lip against pressing me further as she guided me inside. The house smelled like apples and cinnamon, like childhood, like home. "I made your favorite," she shared, pointing to the muffins fresh from the oven. There were also eggs, sausage, and fresh fruit. She loved to put out a spread when we all came over to eat. "We'll eat when Emmie gets here."

"Mason not home from school this weekend?" I asked after my youngest brother. Mason had bucked family tradition and wasn't interested in the club. Instead, he was playing college football. Despite Pop being the former prez and the club having been his life, he respected Mason's choice and supported him. We all did.

"Next weekend," she replied. "You're going to his game, aren't you?"

"Of course," I replied, stealing a muffin and taking a massive bite as she slapped my hand with a laugh.

"Where's Pop?" I asked with my mouth full.

"Working on his bike in the garage."

"I'll go see if I can help him out." I nodded as she handed me two coffees to take with me.

"You tell him breakfast is in twenty, and I know damn well he already stole half of my first batch!" she hollered after me.

I merely chuckled, used to their banter, and headed for the garage. I found my pop squatted beside his bike, his hands and white tee stained with grease as he worked intently on his Harley. It was a familiar sight from my childhood, and I grinned, watching as he swore at the wrench in his hand.

"Need a hand?" I offered with a chuckle.

"You think your old man can't fix his own bike?" he demanded, though his blue eyes were lit with humor. We both knew I wouldn't doubt it for a second. At close to seventy, my pop still operated as though in his prime. And, if the women in town were any testament, the opposite sex still found him more than a little attractive. Fortunately, he'd only ever had eyes for my mom. He treated her like a queen, always had.

"You guys have a good trip?" I asked, handing him his coffee before sitting down on a nearby stool. They'd been traveling abroad.

He nodded. "Beautiful country, but you know me, I always like comin' home."

My mom was the one with the travel bug. He went along to make her happy, and because he'd never let her go alone. But I knew he'd be just as content to stay in Hawthorne.

"Cole tells me you're off your game," he commented in his typical no-nonsense tone. "That you're angry and not yourself."

"I'm all right," I replied, providing my standard response.

He turned his gaze toward me. "Don't give me that bullshit, son. What's eatin' you?"

I looked off to the side, unsure how to answer him. I'd always been able to talk to him about anything. But I wasn't so sure I could talk to him about this.

"You always looked out for everyone before yourself," he began when I didn't respond. "You protected your sister. You were so fucking young, but you took that on as though it was your responsibility to own, even at seven years old. It took us years to get you to trust us to take care of her."

I remembered that time well. My mother hadn't been fit to take care of us. At four, Emmie couldn't fend for herself, so I'd stepped up. I'd taken care of her until Cal and Jill had rescued us. It didn't strike me as anything remarkable; it was what any brother should do.

"You took all the kids under your wing at the club. You were older, but it wasn't so much that. It was just your nature to do so. You've always been quiet, Max," he continued. "You work hard, keep your head down, and do the right thing. But I've always worried that your need to put everyone else first means that you always come a distant second and that might catch up with you some day. Instinct is tellin' me that day is today, so why don't you get that shit off your chest and let your old man help?"

I rubbed a hand over my face. "I wish it were that simple." I took a deep breath. "I want someone I can't have. I'm all fucked up over it."

"What isn't simple about it?"

"It's Wren."

To his credit, he didn't flinch. He didn't even look all that surprised. "And what's holding you back? What Sal will think? That it might hurt him? What about what you want, Max? For once, put yourself first and take what you want."

I eyed him in surprise. "You think it's that simple?"

He shrugged. "Maybe not. But nothing good ever is. Sal is more overprotective than most, I'll give you that. He even gives Cole a run for his money in that department." He chuckled. Grace was constantly fighting with Cole from everything over what she wore to the rare occasions she dared to date, and she was older than Wren.

"Wren's his daughter," he continued. "His only child. But ultimately, all any father wants is for his daughter to find a man who will love her and take care of her. Sal respects you, Max. He loves you like family. You may just have to put in some work to get him to see that you're that man for her."

"You don't seem surprised by all this."

He chuckled. "She's always had feelings for you, son. Was clear as day from the very first. You, you were harder to read, but that's always been the case."

"What about the age difference?"

He eyed me as though I was missing something obvious. "If that had held me back, I wouldn't be married to your mom. Sounds to me like you're making excuses."

Fuck, was he right?

"You need to make a choice," he told me firmly. "Is she your woman or not? Because if she is, then you need to claim her and fuck all the rest. It will sort itself if you face it like the man you are. If she isn't? Then, Max, you need to cut her loose. From the way she's always looked at you, the cruelest thing you could do is leave her hangin', and that's not the way we raised you."

I scrubbed my hand over my hair in agitation. "I think I've already done that. I fucked up with her."

"Well then, you have an uphill battle to fight, don't you?" he challenged. "You may still have her heart, but it doesn't mean she trusts you with it. My advice? Don't give her space. She'll want it because it's safe, because you haven't fought for her until now. Likely no man has. You want her? You need to be the man who does." He turned back to his bike, letting his words sink in.

I stood up taller with a new resolve to do exactly that. "Thanks, Pop."

"Don't mention it. Now go get me one of those muffins your mom made, would ya? Givin' all this advice made me hungry."

I chuckled, not surprised by the request. "She's already pissed you powered through the first batch."

"I love to get that woman riled," he admitted with a gleam in his eye.

I shook my head at him as I made my way back to the kitchen, feeling lighter than I had in months. I'd been trying to protect Wren from what being with me might mean, but it was time to say fuck it and face the music because a life without her just wasn't an option. I'd made my choice—hell, I'd made it years ago and just hadn't admitted it.

It was time to get my girl.

# Chapter 11

The familiar sound of rock n' roll music, low hum of conversation, and bottles clinking met my ears as I walked into the dimly lit Mad's Monday evening. Axel's bar, named after his oldest son, Maddox, was on the outskirts of town. It was a biker bar through and through, and not a place frequented by your typical passing tourist. The few times someone had stumbled in on accident had been downright comical.

Olivia, Emmie, and Grace had convinced me to come out for a drink to celebrate my first day of work. Despite the rowdy environment and occasional fist fight, we all felt completely at home here. It probably had something to do with the fact that if anyone ever laid a hand on us or looked at us sideways, they'd lose a limb, and everyone knew it.

I'd debated hiding at home, potentially under the bed if I wanted to be dramatic about it. The mind-numbing kiss and immediate rejection from Max were still forefront of my mind. But I was determined to move on, and that meant continuing with life as I otherwise would, even if that meant risking running into him.

I forced myself not to scan the bar for him as I walked through. It was a useless exercise anyway. I always seemed to be able to sense him regardless. For the moment, it appeared I was in the clear and made my way to the table in the back where the girls were sharing a pitcher. With a quick wave to Gunner who was tending bar, I plopped down in the empty seat next to Em.

"So, how was it?" Liv asked as she poured me a beer after we'd greeted each other.

"Good." I nodded. The local auto shop where I'd started as a receptionist and mechanic had been in business for as long as I could remember. Despite offers to work for the club, I'd declined, needing to make my own way. "The only awkward part was that apparently my dad came in there to warn all the guys to keep their hands to themselves." I rolled my eyes but really wasn't all that surprised. What had surprised me and what I didn't share was that apparently Max had done the same thing.

"Sounds about right," Grace grumbled. "Thank God I work at a salon, otherwise my dad would have done the same damn thing."

"They mean well, but dammit if it isn't annoying," Liv commiserated with a short laugh.

"Should we get another round?" I offered, pointing to the empty pitcher.

Emmie nodded in agreement. "Gunner! Another round!" she called.

"Get your ass over here and get it," he griped.

She rolled her eyes and stood up with a huff.

"Gunner still likes to get under her skin, huh?" I raised a brow toward Gracie.

"Unfortunately," she muttered. "Those two are like oil and water."

Emmie had just returned with a full pitcher when I felt the energy in the bar change. The conversations buzzing around us grew muted, and the men at the bar visibly straightened, their gazes locked toward the front door.

Max.

I didn't even need to turn around to confirm it was him. I just knew.

"Max and Cash just walked in," Gracie confirmed, looking over my shoulder.

"Great," Emmie grumbled. "Max has been so pissy lately. I have no idea what's up his ass."

"Maybe he needs to get laid," Gracie shrugged as Olivia nearly choked on her drink, sliding a pointed look in my direction.

I looked down at my beer as Grace patted her on the back, oblivious to our exchange.

"Ew, can we not talk about my brother's sex life?" Emmie complained. "And anyway, I don't think that's it. That chick at Gunner's party was all over him, and he blew her off. He's always been picky, but I can't even remember the last time he showed interest in anyone."

I tried not to be thrilled by this news. It would be a long time, if ever, when I could stomach the idea of Max with someone else.

"Ladies," Cash greeted, the ever-present toothpick between

his lips. Cash was a giant Viking of a man with blond hair that fell past his chin and blue eyes. He'd patched in while I was away at school, and though I didn't know him well, it was clear he'd become close with Gunner and Max. He was also gorgeous, I couldn't help but acknowledge despite being completely consumed by Max.

"Hey, Cash," Gracie greeted.

I kept my back to them, forcibly controlling my breath as Max moved into my periphery. "Wren, there's something I need to catch you up on." His voice was low and full of authority.

I ground my teeth. He was putting me on the spot. If I declined, everyone would know something was up. Well, two could play that game.

I forced myself to look up at him. "You caught me up Friday night, remember?" I replied, keeping my tone as light as possible.

His eyes flashed. "There are some key details we didn't get to," he ground out.

"What are you guys talking about?" Emmie asked in confusion.

*Shit.*

"Wren's helpin' me fix up the GTO," he answered easily. Max had a gorgeous black Pontiac GTO. I'd never ridden in it, but had salivated over it for years.

At least one of us could think quickly on their feet.

I eyed him steadily. "I was trying to convince Max not to sell it, but apparently he doesn't think she's worth much."

"Actually," he argued as he continued to stare at me, "she's just about the most important thing to me."

My heart hammered in my chest at his words as my anger flared. "That's quite a change of heart," I observed coolly as the blood ran hot in my veins.

"Not a change." He shook his head. "Call it a realization."

"Why do I feel like we're not talking about a car?" Gracie stage whispered.

In a likely failed bid to downplay our exchange, I turned to Grace with a forced smile. "It's just a car, and speaking of which, I have an early day tomorrow. I should get going. Thanks for the drink." I held up my beer, finishing the dredges and slamming it on the table harder than I'd intended.

Olivia shot me a look that promised she'd be calling me later as I grabbed my jacket and hightailed it out of there.

I heard Max's heavy footfall behind me and winced at the sound.

"Max, a word." Axel's deep baritone was full of urgency, and I knew from experience, it would stop any of the guys in their tracks.

I sent a silent thank you to whatever divine intervention was saving my backside as I barreled out to my car, alone.

I fired up my gorgeous Mustang, very recently street ready, loving the sound of her throaty throttle as I backed out of the lot and onto the road, headed for home.

I decided to take the back way, wanting to clear my head before I had to deal with the nightly twenty questions from my parents. They meant well, but living under their roof was definitely a short-term solution for me.

When a pair of headlights appeared in my rearview far closer than was standard, at first, I blew it off as some asshole on the road. I slowed down to let them pass. Instead, they moved closer to my bumper, the large vehicle bearing down on me with alarming speed.

"What the hell?" I asked out loud as the headlights grew so close I braced for impact. I couldn't get a clear make on the car but could tell it was some sort of large SUV or Suburban. I hit the gas, mindful of the windy road. I was an excellent driver, but my car was old and far smaller than the beast behind me.

I'd thrown my purse with my phone inside into the back seat, far out of reach.

I was on my own.

The steering wheel shook under my hands as I pushed my Mustang to her limits. It felt like an eternity since I'd left the bar but had only been minutes as I began to crest the hill that would drop down toward my parents' house. Sweat broke out on my brow. I was so close to home and so infinitely far.

Who the hell was behind me? What did they want?

My relief at hitting the top of the hill was short lived as a second later the SUV's onslaught intensified and they made contact, hitting my rear end with enough force to send me spinning over the guardrail and off the road into the ravine below. My car crashed through the underbrush as if in slow motion. There was a moment where the nightmare enveloped me until there was just darkness and, oddly, peace.

# Chapter 12

## MAX

*Are you with Wren?*

The text from Olivia had a chill shooting down my spine as I swung off my bike. I'd just pulled into my garage but was quickly ready to ride out again, to where I wasn't sure.

Instead of texting her back, I called her, my phone in a vice grip as I held it to my ear.

"What's going on?" I barked the minute she picked up.

"Wren never made it home from the bar," she told me in a shaky voice. "Sal called me. I was wondering if maybe she went to your place or something."

"No," I replied, wishing like hell she had. A million possibilities rushed through my mind, none of them good. "She left the bar, what, an hour ago?" I asked. "Did she have more than one beer?"

"Just the one, she was fine," she replied. "And yeah, it was about an hour ago. I think Sal and my dad are going to head out and look for her."

"I'll join them. Riding out now," I confirmed, already swinging my leg back over my bike.

I debated where to head first, feeling helpless. The thought of anything happening to Wren had my gut so twisted it was painful as I sped back toward the bar, planning to retrace her steps.

I tried to put myself in her shoes once I got close. She'd been keyed up when she left. Knowing Wren and how much she loved that 'Stang, she might have wanted to take the long way. I immediately pointed my bike toward Raven's point, the windy road that would drop her down toward her parents' place.

I forced myself to go slow, to watch for any clue as to what might have happened. When I hit the crest and saw the guardrail had been busted what looked like recently, the blood chilled in my veins. I cut to the side of the road and swung off my bike, rushing to the edge. When I saw her taillights peeking out through the brush, I let out a roar of fear, sliding down the embankment as fast as my body could go.

"Wren!" I hollered her name, ignoring the vines that cut my face and the rocks that dug into my limbs as I scrambled down the steep ravine.

The sight of her slumped over the wheel was something I'd never forget, not if I lived a thousand years. I reached for my phone, praying it hadn't fallen out in my slide down the hill, relieved to find it still inside my pocket.

"911 what is your emergency?"

"I'm at the bottom of Raven's Peak, my girl went off the road in her car. She's unconscious. I need an ambulance now!" I hollered, my voice shaking with adrenalin and something I wasn't accustomed to feeling—fear.

"Ambulance is in route." The response was immediate. "Were airbags deployed?"

"It's a classic car, no airbags," I rasped, barely able to get the words out as I looked at her delicate frame slumped unnaturally over the wheel.

"Don't move her, sir. They're on their way."

"Did you hear that, baby?" I asked her hoarsely. "They're comin' okay? And I'm here. You're gonna be okay," I told her, my eyes blurring. I couldn't remember the last time I'd cried, but the thought that my sweet girl could have a broken neck or worse was more than I could bear. "There's so much I haven't told you yet. You don't even understand that you're mine." I talked to her through the broken driver's side window. "But you will. You're gonna be fine. I'll make sure of it," I assured her just as much as myself.

I put my phone back to my ear, my hands shaking and bloody from my haste to get to Wren. There was one other call I needed to make.

"Sal? Yeah, I found her."

∗   ∗   ∗

The next hour was complete chaos. The paramedics arrived in record time, but making their way down the hill had been slow going. Getting Wren back up on a backboard was even slower.

I'd ridden alongside her in the ambulance as they took her vitals. She had a huge laceration on her head, but other than that, it was difficult to tell what else might be wrong. I was able to hold her hand, hers so small and delicate in mine.

Sal and Kat were out front of the emergency room when we came in, but were only able to see Wren for a moment before she was rushed off.

Now, we waited.

Most of the club and their women and children had arrived. We took up almost the entire waiting room. I paced, waiting for news.

"Was she drinking?" Sal demanded of Liv.

"She had one beer. She was fine," she told him the same thing she'd told me.

"She's a great driver," Sal muttered to himself, as though trying to piece it all together.

"Sal, man, there were two sets of skid marks," Axel shared, the desire for vengeance clear in his countenance.

I hadn't even noticed. I'd been so consumed with getting to Wren.

"What the fuck?" I roared, knowing I was drawing attention to myself by showing how much I cared and not giving a single fuck. "Someone ran her off the road?"

"Might have," Axel replied, giving me a perplexed look.

"Max, you should get those cuts looked at," my mom put in gently. Gunner and Cole had already tried to get me to do the same.

"Later," I ground out. I wasn't gonna be anywhere but here when the doctor showed up.

I'd nearly worn a hole in the floor by the time the doctor appeared. Kat and Sal shot to their feet. "Mr. and Mrs. Armstrong?" he called, looking at his clipboard. "Would you like to talk in private?" he asked, appraising the room full of bikers.

"Here is fine," Sal ground out, clearly anxious for news.

"Your daughter is stable," he shared, and the news nearly had me collapsing with relief. "She suffered a skull fracture, but X-rays aren't showing any swelling of the brain, which is a very good thing. She has two cracked ribs and some severe bruising, but all in all, I'd count her very lucky, especially considering the lack of safety features in the car."

I made a mental note to forbid her from driving anything without top-of-the-line safety features from this moment forward.

"Unfortunately, other than managing her pain, there's not much we can do, but I'd like to keep her here for observation for the next day or so."

"Can we see her?" Kat asked anxiously.

He nodded. "I'll take you back there."

I moved to follow, ruled my instinct to be with Wren, when a firm grip on my arm blocked my progress. "Not now, son."

Everything in me wanted to argue with my pop, to shove his hand back and follow them.

"I know you're in your own personal hell, but this is their child," he coaxed, his eyes on Kat and Sal. Fear and anguish were written all over their faces as they rushed to follow the doctor. "This isn't the time." His words were firm but gentle as he wrapped an arm around my shoulders, giving me a gentle squeeze.

I took a deep breath and nodded. He was right. Out of respect to them, I'd wait, for now.

It was hours later. Visiting hours were long over, but I couldn't bring myself to leave. I'd crammed my body into a tiny-ass chair, my arms crossed at the chest as I dosed off and on alongside the other poor souls in the same position.

"Why are you still here?" Sal's voice was accusing as he woke me from a restless sleep.

"Sal." Kat placed a gentle hand on his arm in a bid for calm.

His nostrils flared. "No, I want to know why he's still here and why the fuck Wren is asking for him when she's barely conscious."

The fact she'd asked for me had my heart pounding in my chest.

"This isn't the time," I replied, trying like hell to keep my voice calm.

"This isn't the time for what?" He glowered, leaning over me menacingly. I remained seated, knowing if I stood it would only serve to escalate the situation.

"To tell you that I'm in love with Wren," I shared.

His fist flew at my face, making contact with bone-crunching force. My head whipped back, stars blinding my vision as I righted myself, staring up at him calmly. He clenched my jacket in his fists as rage burned in his eyes tinged with anguish.

"I love her, Sal," I repeated quietly, prepared to take anything he had to give. I'd take it for her and for him. "I haven't touched her. Out of respect for you, I wanted to talk man-to-man."

"Man-to-man?" he demanded. "She's a fucking kid! You're way too old for her!" he bellowed as hospital security came in to investigate.

"We're fine," I growled at them, telling them in no certain terms to beat it. They looked uncertain for a moment before making a hasty retreat.

I turned back to Sal, ready to take his anger, all of it. "I love her."

He shoved me back. "You keep saying that," he grumbled, rubbing his fingers through his hair.

"It's true." I shrugged. "It will always be true."

Somehow, I knew that without a doubt.

"This is why you insisted on handling the Portland business," he surmised.

I nodded. "I want to protect her. I want to take care of her."

"She know that?" he demanded, and I swore Kat was fighting a smile behind him.

I shook my head. "She's pretty pissed at me actually. I pushed her away. I was worried about what it might do to you, to your relationship with her. But I love her, and I need her to know it."

He let me go, taking a step back with a grumbled "fuck." He strode out of the hospital, leaving Kat staring at me with a mixture of concern and revelation.

She sat beside me with a watery laugh. "Well, you really did it now, didn't you?"

"Yep." I grunted, touching my eye with a wince. It'd be a hell of a shiner, but I'd had worse.

"She's been quiet lately, withdrawn. That your fault?" she asked.

"Maybe," I admitted regretfully. "I thought I was doing the right thing."

She nodded thoughtfully.

"Now she's lying in there in pain and thinks I don't want her," I rasped in torment.

"She's stubborn like her father, but I'd imagine, you work hard enough, they'll both come around," she shared. "Knowing Sal, he'll need to cool off for a bit." She eyed the hallway that led to Wren's room meaningfully.

I jumped to my feet in a rush to take her up on her wordless offer.

"Max." Her voice stopped me in my tracks. "Sal might be tough and all, but if you hurt her, he's got nothing on a mother's rage. You get me?"

I met her gaze with respect, knowing she meant every word. Behind every Knight, there was a badass female, including mine. "I get you." And with that, I rushed down the hall, ignoring the nurse's call of protest about visiting hours. Nothing was going to keep me from my girl. Not ever again.

# *Chapter 13*

I wasn't sure what had woken me. My pounding head and aching side? The rhythmic beeping of the machines all around me? My eyelids felt like they weighed a hundred pounds as I forced them open to survey the darkened room. I wasn't sure what I'd expected, but the sight of Max bent over, his head laying against my bed fast asleep, wasn't it. His arm was wrapped around my legs as though shielding me even in sleep.

I must have made some sort of movement, because he jerked awake so fast it was nearly comical. "Are you okay?" he asked blearily, looking ready to take on Goliath should he desire a fight just then. Or maybe he'd already fought him. His face was covered in scratches, and he was sporting a hell of a black eye.

"What happened to you?" I asked hoarsely, my throat like sandpaper.

His eyes roamed my face. "I'm fine and so fucking glad to see you breathing, babe." His voice was thick with emotion as his head dropped into my lap. My fingers traveled into his thick head of hair on their own accord. "When I saw your taillights sticking out of that ravine, my heart fucking stopped." His admission was slightly muffled as his face remained pressed to my bedsheets.

"My dad said you found me," I murmured. "I thought I'd heard your voice talking to me. I just figured I was dreaming."

He lifted his head to look at me. "I should have never let you leave the bar like that, upset and without knowing how I feel about you. The thought that you could have been taken from me without knowing how insanely in love with you I am guts me, Wren."

I knew my eyes were wide as saucers as I stared at him in shock. "You're in love with me?"

"Insanely." He made sure to add with a sad smile. "Don't forget that part."

"How...? What?" My foggy brain scrambled to keep up with this sudden change of heart. "I'm not worth it, remember?" I reminded him, sadly turning my head away. The sight of him there was too much for my pain-wracked body to handle.

He squeezed my leg gently. "I never said that, and I never believed it. I don't want you worried about anything now. I just need you to know that I'm here and I'm not going anywhere."

"But my dad... Everyone will know...." I trailed off in confusion.

"Your dad already knows," he confirmed. "I think my trying to break down the door to get to you might have given me away," he added dryly.

I turned to look at him, his injuries making much more sense now. "The black eye," I surmised with a sigh. "Was it bad? What are all those scratches from?"

"Let's just say my trip down the ravine to get to your car wasn't exactly slow or cautious. It's nothing I can't handle. I don't want you to be worried. Everything's gonna be fine."

The fact that he'd been hurt because of me made my heart clench.

"How's your pain?" he asked.

"Okay," I lied.

He eyed me shrewdly. "I'm getting the nurse."

I didn't respond and instead watched his powerful body move across the room in consternation. Had he really said he loved me or had the pain meds created that fantasy?

Rather than question it, as soon as the nurse upped my dose, I let it all go, drifting off into oblivion.

∗   ∗   ∗

When I opened my eyes again, sun was shining through the window and Max was nowhere to be found. Instead, both of my parents were seated at my bedside.

Maybe it all had been a dream after all.

My mom was up in an instant, leaning over me, her hand pressed to my forehead gently, the way she'd always done when I was sick as a kid. My dad's worried face appeared at her side as they both peered down at me.

"How you feeling, honey?" she asked gently.

"Okay," I mumbled groggily. Even if I was in excruciating

pain, I didn't think I'd share it just then. They looked worried enough. "What time is it?"

"Just after noon," she replied.

"Wow so late." I tried to sit up and immediately winced at the pain in my ribs. Which were cracked, right. The extent of my injuries the doctor had explained to me last night came back in a rush.

"You've got to take it really easy, honey," she reminded me as I gave up trying to resituate myself with a frustrated huff.

I looked to my dad, who still hadn't spoken. His jaw was clenched, eyes dark with fury as he watched me struggle to get comfortable. "We're gonna find out who did this, Wren. Do you hear me?"

I nodded mutely, momentarily stunned by the harsh timber of his voice. I'd seen him angry in the past, but never anything like this.

"The entire club was here last night to make sure you were okay," my mom put in gently. "Most of them are back today. We're all so glad you're okay, baby." She swallowed hard, and I knew she was close to tears.

My dad's arm wrapped around her, pulling her in for comfort.

"Everyone is here?" I hedged. I didn't want to outright ask about Max in case I'd imagined our whole conversation.

My mom shot me a knowing smile. "Max was here all night. He went to get us some coffees. Your father's just taking some time to adjust to this new development," she whispered with a playful wink as my dad growled irritably.

"That makes two of us." I sighed. "But whatever it is or isn't, I'm an adult." I looked at my dad pointedly. "Whether you see that or not. And besides, if there is something"—I was too cautious to hope—"wouldn't you rather it be someone you know and trust?" I asked. "Rather than some stranger?"

My mom shot him a pointed look, and I got the impression she'd said the same thing to him. I wasn't surprised; she'd always liked Max.

"How about we just wait a few more years on all of this?" he grumbled. The sad thing was, he was only partially kidding.

"I know you want me to be happy," I replied gently. "I just need you to trust my judgment, regardless of whoever I end up with."

He leaned over me, swiping his big hand over my forehead. "You deserve the world, baby." He gave me a sad smile. "I'm just not sure anyone deserves you. Someday, when you're a mama, you'll understand how I feel."

A moment later, Max strode in to the room, balancing three coffees. He looked exhausted and stunningly handsome in the clothes I remembered him wearing last night. He handed a coffee to both my parents before he took the chair by my side as though he had every right to be there. "Okay?" he asked quietly, his dark eyes sweeping over me with concern.

"I'm okay. Did you ice that shiner?" I asked, shooting a brief glare at my dad. I couldn't believe he'd actually hit him. Then again, knowing him, I absolutely could.

It looked worse today. Coupled with the scratches scattered across his face and neck, he looked like he'd been through the ringer.

He shrugged indifferently, which meant no. "I'm fine."

I sighed in frustration but knew getting on his case wouldn't do anything. "Did they pull my car out yet?" I asked, already wondering how much work I'd have to do to her to get her back running. I'd just gotten her back after working on her nearly every day since I'd been home. I loved that car.

"Yeah, and you're never drivin' it again," Max declared.

"What the hell are you talking about?" I exclaimed in indignation.

"Part of the reason you're injured so bad is because that car had no fuckin airbags and a lap belt." He growled. "You could have been killed. Fix up the 'Stang all you want, but I'm putting you in a Highlander as soon as you're up to driving again."

"A Highlander?" I screeched, looking in frustration at my mom and dad in a foolish bid for support. My dad was watching Max with begrudging approval, which made my blood boil further.

Dear God, there were two of them.

"Don't worry about the car right now," Max continued smoothly. "Can you tell us what happened last night?" he asked, his tone noticeably softer.

"We are talking about it later," I told him firmly. There was no way I was giving in that easily. "As for last night, I really have no idea," I admitted. "This big SUV started following me as soon as I left the bar. At first, I thought they wanted to pass me, so I slowed down, but they only sped up. I couldn't get to my phone, so I just hit the gas. When I hit the top of the hill, they hit me, and I spun out." I swallowed hard, remembering the fear and utter helplessness of that moment. "I hit the guardrail and went down. I don't remember anything after that. Do you think this has to do with what happened in Portland?"

"We don't know," my dad replied, "but we're gonna find out. In the meantime, I don't want you to worry."

I nodded, feeling drained even by the short exchange.

"You need to rest," Max surmised gently.

"So do all of you," I murmured. "Why don't you go home? Get some sleep? I'm fine here," I assured them.

"So am I," he responded easily. "I'll leave when you do, which might be as early as tonight."

I perked up a bit at that. "Really?"

"Really," he confirmed with a soft smile. "Get some sleep."

I sank further into the pillow, my eyes sliding shut.

# Chapter 14

"Outside," Sal snarled at me after Wren fell asleep. I nodded, standing to follow him. I looked to Kat expectantly. I wanted to make sure Wren wouldn't be alone.

"I'm staying," she assured me with a soft smile.

Sal was pacing in the hallway when I closed the door behind me. I was ready for him to rail me again about my intentions with Wren, but his mind was elsewhere. "What the fuck is going on?" he demanded.

I leaned back, one boot on the wall, my arms crossed. "Not sure," I answered honestly. "The Blue Devils have a guy inside Portland PD. They haven't found the man who attacked her—no surprise there," I muttered. "We still can't be sure if the notes she was getting and that attack are the same person. She hasn't gotten anything new, right?"

He shook his head, his jaw clenched. I knew he was as frustrated as I was—probably a little scared too. I knew I sure as hell was. When it came to Wren, I could admit that.

"We need a meet." Sal nodded, already pulling out his phone, I assumed to text my brother.

"Catch me up," I replied evenly, knowing I was risking invoking his anger and not caring in the least. I told her I wasn't leaving, and I'd meant it.

He assessed me warily. "You want to stay with Wren." It wasn't a question.

"I'm staying." I dared him to challenge me.

He blew out a slow breath, looking off to the side a moment before his gaze returned to me. "Fine. We'll catch you up." And with that, he strode away without another word.

I watched him go, knowing that to some, his reaction would seem cold, but I knew Sal, and that right there was progress.

When Wren was discharged that night, everything in me protested her not being with me, but I knew I'd have to work up to that. For now, the important thing was that she was safe. After telling her I'd see her soon, the confusion on her face making it all the more clear how much work I had to do, I left her in the care of her parents and headed home to catch a shower and change clothes.

Cole had caught me up on their earlier meet. There was still no new information, and that wasn't fucking good enough. It seemed like I'd be making another trip to Portland.

* * *

"He's dead."

Gunner's tone was low as he shared the news with me that Wren's attacker had been killed. "Once you told me you wanted to go back down to Portland, I started digging around. Looks like he was killed a few days ago." He looked up at me, a solemn look in his eye. "Car accident."

"What the fuck?" Cole demanded. "That can't be a coincidence."

"Nope," I agreed, my heart hammering in my chest. "Why the fuck haven't the Devils told us about this?"

Cole eyed me thoughtfully. "You don't trust them?"

"Right now, beyond the members of this club, I don't trust shit." I grunted.

"Last thing we need is a war with another club," Cole muttered, sitting back in his chair. "Been through one of those before, not eager to relive it." He was referring to the war the club had with the Black Riders when I was just a kid.

"I don't want it to come to that," I agreed. "But if we find out they knowingly held back information...." I trailed off darkly.

"We'll be having more than words," he growled.

"I need a fucking beer." Gunner grunted, rising from his seat and striding off to the fridge we kept stocked.

"You look like shit," Cole noted with his typical no-nonsense manner.

"Thanks." I chuckled dryly.

He cocked his head to the side. "Sal have a good reason to clock you?"

"Depends on what your definition of a good reason is." I shrugged, knowing Cole was just as protective of Grace as Sal was of Wren, sometimes more so.

"You made a play for Wren," he surmised.

I looked over at him in surprise. "Pop tell you that?"

He shook his head. "Lucky guess. Looks like he took it about as well as I'd expect."

"Better, actually," I replied honestly. I'd expected worse.

"This gonna cause an issue?"

"No," I replied, hoping that was true.

He eyed me thoughtfully. "Good." He stood up just as Gunner returned with three beers. "I'm good," Cole declined. "Gotta get home to Scarlet. She smells way better than you assholes." He snorted before turning to look at me. "Knowing Sal, he'll come around. He's just a stubborn motherfucker sometimes. In the meantime, put some ice on that shiner." He slapped my back with an amused chuckle before heading toward his bike.

Gunner handed me a beer, keeping the other two for himself. "Glad words out, man. I suck at keeping secrets." He grimaced, taking a pull from his beer. "Hope after all this, she actually wants your ugly ass."

I shot him an annoyed look, despite the fact that I hoped the same damn thing.

# Chapter 15

"Wren, honey, are you going to put that poor man out of his misery or should I take him out back and shoot him?" my mom quipped as she sat gently on my bed.

It had been a week since I'd been home from the hospital, and Max had come over every day, staying for hours despite my not wanting to see him, despite what I was sure had to be a chilly reception from my dad.

I wasn't trying to be cold to Max; I was just confused and in pain and hadn't felt equipped to handle this apparent change of intention from him. If I was being honest, I was terrified of having him let me down.

"He's still down there, huh?" I asked as I lay flat on my back staring at the ceiling. It wasn't comfortable to do much else, and I was already dealing with a serious case of cabin fever. I couldn't imagine another month or more like this.

"Has been for hours," she confirmed. "Between you and your father both being so damn stubborn, I have to admit, I didn't expect him to crack first." She grinned playfully.

I looked at her in surprise.

She shrugged. "He's not at the point of admitting it yet, but I think he likes having Max around. They've been working a bit on that old Chevy he bought." She wrinkled her nose. She hated that car. "And I don't think he minds having another eye on the house, especially when he wants to run out for a bit. But most importantly, Max is proving he's serious about you. I think your dad remembers a bit about what that was like when we first got together."

She got a dreamy look in her eye—the one she always got when she talked about my dad. "I don't want to push you," she continued gently. "I'll support whatever you want to do, but I think whatever doubts your feeling, talking to him might be the first step."

"You're right," I replied with a resigned sigh. "Plus, I don't think he's going anywhere until I actually talk to him."

She squeezed my leg. "I don't think so either."

"All right," I agreed. "I look like shit but not much I can do about it." I grimaced. I didn't have a stitch of makeup on, my hair was greasy, and I'd been wearing the same ratty T-shirt for days. "If this doesn't scare him away, nothing will," I joked, gesturing to my appearance.

"You're beautiful," she assured me as only a mother could. "I'll go get him."

My heart began to pound in anticipation as she left the room. I listened with intent to her quiet tread on the stairs and then, moments later, his much louder one as he made his way closer.

When a quiet tap on the door sounded, followed by him entering the room, I was momentarily speechless at the sight of him. Dressed in his trademark blue jeans and black tee, his hair mussed and luminous eyes trained on me, it was hard to remember how to breathe. My dowdy appearance suddenly felt that much worse, and I longed for a black hole to rise up and swallow me.

"So, you survived the wrath of Sal Armstrong, huh?" I quipped, trying to hide my sudden onslaught of nerves.

A ghost of a smile crested his lips, but his gaze was clouded with concern. "How are you?" I'd always loved that deep voice of his.

"Everything considered, I'm okay," I replied. "I'm looking forward to being able to breathe without pain, but one step at a time."

He stepped further into the room, and I gestured to the side of the bed where my mom had just been. He sat down so cautiously it would have been funny if it wasn't so damn sweet. "You didn't want to see me." It wasn't a question.

So, we were going to get right to it. Knowing Max's personality, I couldn't say I was surprised. He'd never been one for small talk. "I wasn't ready," I amended.

"And you are now?"

"I wouldn't say that." I laughed lightly. "But it doesn't look like you're going away so...."

"You're right," he agreed. "I'm not." He cocked his head to the side. "Do you remember everything I told you at the hospital?"

I nodded.

"That's not changing, Wren, I think you know me well enough to know that I would never say anything like that if I wasn't absolutely serious. I wouldn't be here every day if I wasn't. I admit, I had to work through what it might mean to take this step with you. I want to protect you from everything, even being with me. But you know what? I can't stay away from you. I've been completely fucked up since I started trying. I think you have too."

His eyes searched my face for some glimmer of confirmation, but I was too shocked to give him one. "I want this, more than I've ever wanted anything. Whatever shit it stirs up, we'll be better together. I'm all in, baby. And truth be told, once I shared my intentions and started to deal with the fallout, all I wish is that I'd done it sooner. You wouldn't have doubted me otherwise." He leaned closer, his eyes fierce with intent. "But it was never that I wouldn't fight for you, Wren," he declared adamantly. "I just didn't want you to have to fight for me."

That protective gene in Max ran so deep, always had. It made sense to me that that's what had held him back.

"But I would have," I insisted. "And I can hold my own. Sometimes you have to let people fight their own battles," I told him. "And if that battle happens to be over you, then just know that you're worth it."

His gaze warmed to molten as he searched my face. "You believe that, don't you?"

"I always have," I replied firmly. "Don't you?"

He ran a hand through his hair. "One thing I think I'm realizing through all this," he shared quietly, "is that, despite my parents giving Em and me everything we could have ever wanted, having my mom ditch us fucked me up." He shrugged, looking off to the side as though it pained him to admit that. "I guess I didn't realize that until I actually wanted to give my heart to someone."

I looked at this man who was a heady concoction of ferocity and vulnerability, who didn't share a whole lot but was opening himself to me, and I realized that I wanted to be the woman who made him feel safe to do that, to give his heart to me. Because in that moment, I realized with striking clarity that I loved the hell out of him. And that heart? I wasn't ever giving it back.

I reached over and put my hand over his. "Well, she missed out on a hell of a man," I murmured. "But I don't want to."

His eyes widened with cautious hope. "Yeah?"

"Yeah."

He leaned over, brushing his mouth over mine before pulling back and gently cupping my face with his palm. "I'm gonna make you so fucking happy."

"I know." And I did. Somehow, in that moment with us both laid bare, I knew that.

"As soon as you're up and around, I'm taking you on a real date," he vowed. "But for now, I'll hang here with you."

I looked at him skeptically. "You want to hang out with this grungy-ass girl who can barely move, all with a hostile father downstairs?"

I expected him to laugh or maybe roll his eyes. Instead I was met with an expression so full of determination it rendered me speechless. "Every day. Wouldn't be anywhere else."

"You're a glutton for punishment," I accused gently.

"And you're mine," he replied, as if that explained everything. And hell, in Max's world, it pretty much did.

# Chapter 16

## MAX

"We've got an issue, man," Tank, enforcer for the Blue Devils, told me the next morning. I'd just pulled up in front of Wren's, intent on spending the day with her.

I immediately stiffened, the phone pressed that much harder to my ear. "What's the issue?" I asked gruffly as I leaned against my bike, eyes on Wren's house.

"Went by your girl's old place to give it a final onceover since we moved all their shit out, and fuck, man, there was some pretty weird shit waiting on the front porch."

My blood chilled at his words, and I braced. "Like what?"

"Flowers with a note that says, 'I'm sorry.' A framed picture of your girl that looks like it was taken at a distance, and then a box of dead roses with a note that says, 'Betrayed.' Looks like he got progressively more pissed since my guess is this shit wasn't all delivered at the same time. He probably didn't know she'd left town until recently."

"Fuck," I swore. I could barely hear through the whirring

in my ears as rage blurred my vision. "He ran her off the fucking road," I growled.

"That would be my guess," Tank agreed. "Whoever delivered that shit is pretty twisted."

"And fucking dead," I clipped. "Thanks for the update. I'll be in touch if we need anything, but my guess is that this has moved into Knight's territory." Despite not wanting danger anywhere near Wren, I relished the opportunity to handle this myself. It didn't sit well to have another man, or another club, fight what I considered to be my battle.

"You got it, man," he replied in parting before the line went dead.

For a moment, I sat staring at Wren's house, fighting the urge to drag her back to my place and never let her go. I didn't doubt Sal could keep her safe. Hell, he had the place more secure than a maximum-security prison, but that didn't change the instinct. He and I would be having words, and soon.

I took a deep breath, knowing I needed to calm the hell down as I made my way up their front walk. It was Kat who opened the door, her eyes warm as she gestured me inside.

"How is she today?" I asked, my voice low.

"Better I think," she replied. "Getting out for a short walk would do her good. The doctor wants her to move around a bit. Plus, she's already cranky at being cooped up." She gave me a pointed look as though to say I'd have my hands full. I was more than happy to take on the challenge. "She's upstairs." She gestured toward the staircase.

I nodded and headed that way, anxious to set eyes on my girl after the news from Portland. I tapped on the door lightly before pushing it open, finding Wren half inside a sweatshirt.

I cocked my head to the side, not entirely sure what was going on. "Babe?"

Her body turned toward me in surprise before her shoulders visibly slumped inside the material.

"Are you stuck?" I asked in concern, grateful she couldn't see my lip twitching toward a smile.

"If you laugh, I'll kill you," she grumbled.

"I won't laugh," I promised as I stepped closer. "Let me slide this off," I coaxed as I slid the material up over her head. I crouched low to drop a gentle kiss to her lips. "How about something that zips up the front?"

The deep blush on her cheeks from my kiss was gorgeous as she nodded. "Should have thought of that. What are you doing here anyway?" she asked as I rummaged in her closet, pulling out a soft sweatshirt I'd seen her wear.

"I told you I'd be here every day," I replied, as though it should be obvious.

Her eyes popped wide as I zipped her up. "I didn't think you meant literally."

I cupped her cheek, staring down into her gorgeous eyes. "Well, I did."

"Okay," she breathed. I'd never tire of seeing how obviously I affected her.

"You up for a short walk?" We'd stay close to the house and I'd be armed, a fact I'd keep to myself for now. Wren needed to focus on her recovery, but that didn't mean I wouldn't be sharing with her the need to be cautious. I'd also have to explain why I planned to be that much more overprotective until this situation was dealt with.

"Yeah," she agreed readily. "A couple of days in the house, and I'm getting squirrely."

Damn, she was cute.

She took the stairs slowly as I followed closely behind.

"Okay, honey?" Kat asked when we entered the kitchen, finding both her parents sipping coffee. Sal's jaw clenched as his gaze locked on the grasp I had on Wren's hand, but he remained silent.

"Better I think," Wren replied. "We're just gonna go on a short walk."

"All right, honey." Kat nodded as I guided Wren toward the door.

∗　∗　∗

"Even Corey Harris?" Wren demanded in disbelief as we walked side by side, making slow progress around her block.

"He was a moron, babe," I scoffed.

"So that's a yes," she confirmed incredulously. She'd been listing off every guy she'd had a crush on in school that, as it turned out, I'd chased away at one point or another.

At the time, it hadn't been necessarily intentional, but now that we were going down the list, the evidence was pretty damning.

"You had terrible taste, present company excluded of course." I grinned.

"I was twelve when I liked Corey!" She laughed, smacking my arm.

"Still." I shrugged, dodging her.

"I wish I could have chased off your fan club," she muttered, the sudden sadness in her tone stopping me in my tracks.

I stepped in front of her, stooping to her eye level. "As far as I'm concerned, there was no one before you, understand?" I told her fiercely.

She bit her lip, looking off to the side. "I get that it's ridiculous of me to care and unfair to even say it. Not like I expected you to live like a priest or something."

"There's just you," I murmured. "You're all I see. As far as I'm concerned, those others, they didn't even happen." I meant that too. Every word.

Her expression lightened, and I could tell she believed me. "Okay, Max."

"While we're on the subject though..."

"There hasn't been anyone," she interjected quietly, her cheeks turning pink once again as she picked up on my line of thinking.

I looked down at her in both relief and surprise. I couldn't imagine another man's hand on the girl I'd considered mine for longer than I cared to admit. On the other hand, she was fucking stunning. How she'd kept herself away from men wasn't something I completely understood.

"There just wasn't anyone I was interested in," she continued quietly when I hadn't replied. "No one was you," she admitted so quietly I almost didn't hear her.

But I did, and her whisper might as well have been as loud as a bass drum for the impact it had on me.

If she hadn't been injured, she probably would have been up over my shoulder and on the back of my bike on the way to my place so I could show my gratitude. As it was, I took her mouth in as passionate of a kiss as I dared.

"I'll spend the rest of my life proving I was worth the wait," I vowed against her lips. "I'll be your first and your last."

Her intake of breath was all the gratification I needed as I pulled away reluctantly, capturing her hand and guiding her to what she called home, for now.

*   *   *

"We need to talk," I told Sal the minute Wren went upstairs to take a nap. Even our short walk had worn her out. I'd found him out in the garage under the hood of his latest project.

"Oh yeah?" he asked gruffly.

"Had a call from Tank." I leaned against the doorframe watching him work. "That stalker shit with Wren, it's worse than we thought."

He stood up, his gaze lethal as he gave me his full attention, without words telling me to continue. It was something I'd always liked about Sal. Like me, he didn't say much, but he always made his intentions abundantly clear.

"Tank found multiple deliveries on her front porch. Looks like he got progressively agitated. Not sure why, maybe he saw me with her. I don't have any doubt at this point he ran her off the road and is here in Hawthorne."

"Fuck," Sal clipped. "Why the hell am I just hearing about this now?"

I knew what he meant; he wanted to know why Tank hadn't called him. If there was ever a time to make a claim, it was now. "Because she's mine." I answered firmly. "I under-stand she's your daughter," I continued when he looked ready to speak, "but she's my woman, Sal—my forever. If you don't get that now, you will. But until then, you need to know, I'm not backing down. I'm not stepping back. I'll protect her from everything and anything. If you and I need to come to blows over it, so be it, but I'd rather have your blessing."

He looked to the side a moment, as though considering his next move. "It won't come to blows again unless you give me a good reason," he replied, the threat clear in his tone.

"If I give you reason, then by all means." Hell, if I ever hurt Wren, I'd kneel at his feet and welcome it.

He blew out a breath and nodded slightly, that small chin dip likely the most acknowledgement I'd get for now. "That asshole that attacked her," he said, clearly done with as close to a heart-to-heart as we may ever get, "any chance he could have dropped off those packages before he was killed? Could he be her stalker?"

"I don't think so," I replied, wishing it was that simple. "That's what's bugging me. I'm not sure exactly how yet, but it seems likely the attacker and her stalker are linked. Plus, the way the attacker died is too fucking coincidental."

"You think her stalker killed him?"

"I do." I nodded. "I just don't know why."

"She know any of this yet?"

I shook my head. "Was gonna give her a few more days to rest up, but I plan to tell her. She needs to know, and plus, knowing Wren, she'd be pissed as hell if she found out I kept this from her."

"True."

The silence between us stretched for a moment. "I'll head out for a while, swing back by later," I said finally.

He cleared his throat. "Could use some help with this." He gestured toward the engine of the car he was working on. "If you don't have any place to be," he added gruffly.

I peeled off my cut, throwing it over the chair in the corner, accepting the olive branch he was offering. The truth was, I had a bunch of shit to take care of, but there was nowhere more important for me to be. "I can stay," I assured him, holding out my hand for the wrench. "Let's see what's going on." I nodded toward the old Chevy.

And with that, a fragile truce was made.

# Chapter 17

"You still here?" my dad asked Max gruffly as he walked into the living room that afternoon. It had been over a week, and my dad asked him the same thing every day. It had become a running joke of sorts, one my dad may or may not have seen the humor in.

"Still here," Max replied with a lip twitch as we lay watching a movie on the couch with Olivia sprawled out in the love seat to my right. Max had been reluctant to leave at the end of each day. I kept assuring him I was feeling better, understanding he had a life to take care of, and I felt bad he was so obviously putting it on hold for me. Every day I felt a bit stronger. I'd been able to scale back substantially on my pain meds, though I still longed for the day I could cough without pain.

When both he and my dad's cells went off simultaneously, I knew it had to be club business.

My dad glanced at his text. "Cole wants a meet," he told Max.

Max simply stared at him as a silent standoff of sorts took place between them.

"I'll go," my dad grumbled, grabbing his cut before turning to me. "Your mom's still at Dixie's helping Piper with inventory. She calls, you let her know to call me."

"Will do, Pop," I agreed, knowing something monumental had just happened. My dad had deferred to Max when it came to keeping me safe. That was big. No, it was huge.

He leaned over, placing a quick kiss to the top of my head. "Love you, little bird."

"Love you too." I smiled up at him.

"That felt like sort of a big deal," I murmured as the sound of my dad's Harley could be heard roaring off down the road.

"Totally," Liv agreed.

Max simply squeezed my foot as we settled back into our movie.

"Gracie's salon is having an anniversary party tonight," Liv put in as the credits were rolling. "You guys want to go?"

"Not tonight," Max's response was swift and left no room for argument.

I'd brought up going out more than once but had been shot down every time. I was still recovering, but pretty soon I'd be pushing the subject. I could only stay cooped up for so long.

Liv made a pouty face but said nothing more about it, sensing, as I did, that she wouldn't get anywhere with Max. Not tonight anyway.

Olivia was just getting ready to leave when Max's phone rang. "Gonna take this outside," he muttered, rising to stalk toward the front door, his phone already pressed to his ear.

"Who calls anyone these days anyway?" Liv demanded in bafflement.

I laughed at her befuddled expression. "I wish I could go with you tonight." I pouted as she gathered her jacket and purse.

"Me too." She sighed. "But I'm sure Mr. Alpha will let you out of the house eventually."

"Hopefully," I replied with a dramatic sigh. "I know he's just worried, but starting our dating life with constant chaperones is a total bummer."

She snorted. "I'm sure he's had a case of blue balls for weeks."

I was trying to suppress a laugh when Max strode back in. "You takin' off?" he asked Liv.

She nodded. "Thanks for letting me be a third wheel. I'll text you later," she told me in parting as she waved to us both and made her way for the front door.

"Take pictures tonight and send them to me!" I called after her.

"Will do," she agreed.

"What do you feel like doing?" I asked Max once she was gone.

"That was your pop." He gestured to his phone. "He and Cole are making a run to Vegas. I'm gonna take you to my place."

My eyes popped wide in surprise. The idea of being with Max at his place, alone, was more than welcome, but I worried what could be going on to have my dad agree to it. "What's wrong?"

"It's fine. We have it handled," he assured me. "I'll help you gather up enough of your stuff for a few days."

"A few days?" I squeaked.

He eyed me intently. "If I have my way, it'll be a lot more than that."

I wasn't sure exactly what he meant by that and was maybe a little afraid to ask as he made his way to the stairs headed for my room. My man was on a mission, that was for sure.

I would have protested him basically lifting me into the passenger side of his truck thirty minutes later, but the thing was massive. Even without cracked ribs, I would have had trouble. It was a sweet ride with matte black paint and a black-on-black interior.

"I can't believe I've never been to your house," I marveled as we hit the road.

He shrugged. "Not many people have." This didn't surprise me knowing how much Max liked to keep to himself. The fact that I'd become an exception to that rule wasn't something I'd ever take lightly, or stop reveling in.

"But I get to," I pressed with a small smile.

He looked over at me. "Well, you're my girl." He stated this as fact, and I'd never get tired of hearing him say it. He raised a brow at me. "You just wanted me to say that, didn't you?" he accused with a chuckle.

"I did," I admitted without shame.

He simply shook his head at me as we made our way outside of town, driving well off the beaten path before pulling up in front of a lodge-style home framed by mountains and wilderness.

"Stay there," he ordered as he parked out front, dropping down out of the driver's seat and moving around to my side, lifting me carefully down to my feet. "I bought the place about a year ago," he explained as I took in my surroundings. "I've been fixing it up, but it's still a work in progress," he said as two black mastiffs came bounding in our direction.

I was well acquainted with the breed as Cole and Scarlet had always had one or two, but their size still had me taking a step back.

"Heel," Max ordered as both dogs came to a skidding stop at his feet.

"This is Boulder, but I call him Bo." He pointed to the larger of the two. "And this is his sister, Sky."

I quirked a brow at the names. He'd told me about his animals, but not how they got their names.

"I let Tag's kids name them when they were younger. Fucking *Paw Patrol*," he muttered with an adorably sheepish grin. I had no idea what that was but figured it was some sort of kids show. "That's Frank. He thinks he's a dog." He pointed to a large tabby who was butting its head against my leg.

"Did the kids name him too?"

"I named him," he replied, appearing affronted.

"Oh." I laughed at his expression. "They're cute." I smiled sincerely.

He shrugged. "Gunner's mom breeds Mastiffs. They guard the property. Though I gotta admit, I didn't plan on getting them. They were just so fucking cute I couldn't resist," he admitted, looking nearly bashful and never more gorgeous than he was right in that moment. "And Frank, well, he turned up one day and never left," he shared as we made our way inside.

We walked into a gorgeous great room with vaulted wood ceilings and a killer stone fireplace that went all the way to the ceiling. Floor-to-ceiling windows showcased the view of the mountain range and let in an abundance of sunshine.

"This is gorgeous," I breathed.

"Thanks," he replied, seeming genuinely pleased that I liked it. "Majority of the work that I still have to get to is the kitchen and bathrooms. Cole, Gunner, and Pop have been helpin' me out."

I looked behind him toward the open concept kitchen that, though outdated, looked fully functional. I followed him down a hall as he pointed out an empty room, save for some gym equipment, an office and a master, which was sparsely furnished with a king-sized bed, a bedside table, and a dresser.

"It's sparse." He chuckled as though realizing it for the first time.

I cocked a brow at his understatement. "It's very you," I shared, looking around the space. Despite the lack of furniture, hints of Max were everywhere, from the stack of books on the nightstand to the black frames only a few people even knew he wore for reading, to the scent of peppermint and pine that was just barely noticeable in the air. I looked over at the large king-size bed, unable to stop myself from picturing being tangled up with him there.

As though he could read my thoughts, or was having the same ones himself, he grabbed my hand, leading me back out to the kitchen. "Probably smart to get out of the bedroom."

I didn't agree but followed him nonetheless.

"Make yourself at home. I'm just gonna change my shirt."

He gestured to the grease all over his white tee, a consequence of helping my dad out earlier.

I nodded, watching as he strode back toward the bedroom, admiring his amazing backside as he went. The man sure could fill out a pair of jeans. I sighed dreamily, reaching down to pat Bo's head as he sat at my side watching me with interest. "You don't get many visitors, do you?" I asked him quietly.

Max returned a moment later, wearing a black tee and black jeans. "Sorry, they're a bit needy. I haven't been home much," he admitted, eyeing both dogs, who were now clambering for my attention.

"You've been putting your life on hold to be with me," I concluded, feeling renewed guilt wash over me.

He cocked his head to the side. "Don't you get it, baby? You are my life."

I'd always known Max was intense, but nothing could have ever prepared me for the weight of his stare in moments like this.

"We barely just started dating," I protested. "Isn't it fast?"

He shrugged, undeterred. "So? Did you expect me to put everything on the line for something I wasn't dead serious about?" He looked almost angry now.

He leaned against the counter, eyeing me as I stood across from him. "I don't make decisions lightly." This was something I already knew. "When I make up my mind, I'm all in. And when it comes to being with you, at the end of the day, it was the most freeing decision I've ever made, like gears shifting into place. I'm not gonna play games or beat around the bush. It's just not how I'm made. Now, if you can't handle that, that's another thing entirely."

"I can handle it."

His mouth quirked at my quick response. "That's good, babe. Because honestly? For me, I don't think there'd be any going back."

"Me either," I whispered truthfully. I'd been sure Max was it for me when I was ten years old. Whether or not he'd ever decided the same, I'd have been lost to him for the rest of my life. I knew that instinctively, without doubt. The fact that now I got to be lost in him was just about the very best scenario I could have hoped for.

And I had hoped.

"What do you think about dinner?" he asked, releasing me from the intensity of his gaze.

I had to take a deep breath and shake myself out of it before I could even answer him. "Do you even have anything here?" I asked skeptically.

"Nope." He chuckled, as though realizing it for the first time. "Are you up for going to the store?"

I looked at him incredulously. "Are you kidding? After being laid up, it's sad how excited I am about going to the damn grocery store."

He chuckled. "All right, new plan. Let's hit the store, I'll make you dinner, and then we're going to bed early. Can't tell you how many goddamn weeks I've been waiting to get you in my bed."

My face suffused with heat.

"Just to sleep," he amended, his eyes dropping to my ribs. "For now."

Well, damn.

# *Chapter 18*

MAX

"Why am I not surprised coffee is the first thing you throw in the cart?" I chuckled as Wren marched around the grocery store with purpose. A warm feeling settled in my gut watching her pull items from the shelf to place in our cart to put in our home. She might have thought she was just staying a few days. I had other ideas.

She shrugged. "I'm not ashamed of my caffeine addiction. Other habits I might wait a bit on," she muttered then slapped a hand over her mouth as though she hadn't meant to speak.

"Like what?" I asked, intrigued as I leaned against the cart, pushing it leisurely alongside her.

She blushed, something I loved to make her do. I couldn't wait to find out if that blush went all the way down.

"Come on, babe," I pressed, truly curious now.

"I just like weird stuff—weird combinations of food," she was quick to amend when I shot her a raised brow.

"Like...?" I asked as we made our way down the cereal aisle.

"Like Cheetos and milk," she blurted out. "And honey on pizza. It's actually really good," she defended before I could even say anything. "French fries dipped in honey... I could go on," she said it as though it was a threat, which had me biting back a laugh.

"Wow, so this is a whole thing," I replied, trying hard to sound weirded out rather than flat-out laughing like I wanted to. I had to fuck with her; I couldn't resist. "How did I not know about this?"

"It's not a *thing*," she defended.

I slung an arm around her shoulders, kissing her temple. "I'm just fuckin' with you, babe. I don't care what you like to eat, especially since its working for you so well." I grabbed her ass for emphasis.

"Max!" she exclaimed, darting her eyes around the store, her face bright red.

I pulled her into my side. "I want to know everything there is to know about you. I'll try honey on pizza. Sounds weird as fuck, but if you say it's good, what the hell?"

She shot me an adorable attempt at a glare before marching ahead of the cart, pulling cereal off the shelves as she went.

When she put a couple of dog bones and some catnip in the cart, I raised a brow. "You trying to bribe them?"

"No," she defended. "I just thought they could use a treat."

"That's sweet, baby, but I have some bones at home. Plus, those would be gone in about two seconds," I added, eyeing the tiny bones she'd picked out. "And the catnip, I wouldn't buy that unless you want to be up all night with a crazy-ass cat."

"Oh," she mumbled dejectedly, and I wanted to kick my own ass.

"Tell you what, Frank loves playing with pipe cleaners. We'll get a few more of those, and maybe we'll throw the dogs a few hotdogs as a treat," I bargained.

Her eyes lit up at that, and she nodded.

I wrapped my arm around her and kissed her temple again. "You don't have to give them treats though, babe. They'll love you regardless."

"I just never had pets growing up. I want them to like me, which I realize sounds really stupid." She wrinkled her nose.

"It doesn't, and they will. Now let's get the rest of our shit and hit the road, all right?"

"Sure," she agreed.

An hour later, empty dinner plates beside us, we were sitting on my back deck with beers in hand.

Despite the darkness, I could still smell the pine trees and sense the wide-open space that surrounded my property. After the first few years of my life growing up in such a small house that was never clean, the fresh mountain air was like a balm I never knew I needed.

I didn't think about that time of my life much, but I knew certain decisions I made as an adult were still dictated by how my childhood had begun.

"This is beautiful." Wren sighed contentedly. "Did you always know you wanted this much space?"

I shrugged, taking a sip of my beer, not wanting to get into the details. "Not necessarily, though I knew I wanted to be out of town away from things."

"This is your sanctuary," she deduced, looking affectionately at both dogs sprawled at our feet.

"Never thought about it that way, but I guess you're right," I acknowledged. "I want it to be yours too."

She turned her head to smile at me, looking more relaxed than I'd seen her since her accident. "I could see that happening easily. But, Max," she began somewhat hesitantly, "I miss my friends and being out."

I knew where she was going with this, and knew I'd likely waited too long to lay it out for her.

She emitted a soft growl of frustration, misinterpreting my silence. "I know I'm still sore, but the doctor said its fine," she protested.

"This isn't about what the doctor said," I shared, reaching over to coax her hair behind her ear. "There are some things I was waiting to tell you until you were feeling a bit better."

I watched as dread shuttered her expression. I hated having to put that look on her face. "What?"

"There were more deliveries at your place in Portland. Some more threatening than others. And the guy who attacked you in the parking lot? He was killed—murdered I think."

She sucked in a shocked breath, wincing at the pain in her ribs.

"Fuck, this is why I was waiting to tell you," I ground out. "Do you need some pain killers?"

"No." She shook her head in frustration. "I want to know more about the news that impacts my life that you waited to tell me about," she insisted angrily. "How long have you known about this?"

"About a week."

Her mouth dropped open in surprise. "What else do you know?"

"With the way your attacker was killed, a car accident, I'm sure it was your stalker that ran you off the road. That means he's here in Hawthorne and likely knows where you are too."

"Shit," she breathed as I reached over to take her hand. I could feel her pulse racing under my thumb as I stroked her soft skin.

"Until he's dealt with, I don't intend to let you out of my sight, and in the rare instances where I need to, you'll have a man on you."

"My dad knows this?" she asked woodenly.

"He does."

"So, you two are in cahoots then? I think I liked it better when you weren't getting along," she mumbled, and I was relieved to see some of her trademark sass back in action.

I bit back a smile. "Cahoots? Babe, you've been watching too much *Law and Order*."

She glared at me.

"He's not going to touch a hair on your head," I swore. "But I need you to work with me. I know you're feeling cooped up, but until this blows over, we need to be really fucking careful."

She sighed, and I knew she understood. "Fine, I get that. I wish you would have told me sooner." She paused to give me a pointed look. "But I get it. Still, don't you think we can venture out to the club now and again? To Mad's? Both those places are well protected."

She had a point. I knew there was a good part of me that just wanted to keep her to myself regardless of any danger she was in. But eventually that would make her unhappy, and I'd never want to be the cause of that.

"Yeah, we can do that," I agreed somewhat begrudgingly.

She shot me a warm smile. "Don't worry, honey, we'll spend plenty of nights locking ourselves away from the world like you used to, except now you're stuck with me." She winked.

"Sounds fucking perfect," I replied with conviction, squeezing her hand that was still placed in mine.

"Now that we're getting all this out there, where did my pop go? Should I be worried?" she asked.

I deliberated for only a moment on how much to share. Wren would never be the kind of woman that would accept me keeping things from her. And hell, I didn't want that kind of woman anyway. "We've had some issues with a mafia organization in Vegas." I took a swig of my beer before continuing. "They've started trying to expand their business, running drugs and firearms through our area to get up to Oregon. We're not gonna let that happen."

"Good." She nodded. That was my girl. She didn't complain about the business itself or worry further now that she knew the state of play. She trusted the club, and me, to handle our business. That meant more than I could ever say.

"Things heat up, it'll be more than you that's on lockdown," I shared.

She sighed, looking up at the stars. "Wouldn't be the first time," she pointed out.

"Nope," I agreed as she yawned huge. It had been a big day for her, and I needed to make sure she got enough rest. "What do you say we go to bed?"

She nodded. "That sounds good."

I stood up, pulling her up with me, and guided her inside and down the hall, with the dogs and cat trailing behind us. "I'm gonna shut things down. You go on and get ready."

She nodded sleepily, wandering off down the hall as I watched her hungrily. It was going to be the goddamn challenge of my life to keep my hands to myself, but she was still in pain. I needed to go slow, to be careful, when what I really wanted was to throw her on the nearest surface and pound into her sweet little body until neither of us could breathe.

I shook my head, trying to clear it as I moved around the house, checking the alarms and turning off lights. I moved slowly, letting her have some time to adjust, wanting her to be comfortable and not to crowd her as she got used to my space.

When I wandered back to the bedroom, I nearly laughed out loud. Wren was already passed out under the covers with both dogs and the goddamn cat on the bed.

"Off," I commanded as quietly as possible. The dogs knew they weren't allowed up there and skulked guiltily to their beds on the floor. "You too," I added to Frank, who just eyed me in challenge.

Damn cat.

I picked him up and put him on the floor, knowing he'd just jump back up in a few minutes. Trying to prove who was boss with him was impossible, but I kept trying, fighting a losing battle.

I crawled into bed, wanting to pull Wren into my arms but knowing that could hurt her. For now, I was content to have her in my bed, a place I'd dreamed of her resting her head for so goddamn long I wasn't even sure when the wish had originally been planted.

"Night, baby," I murmured, relishing the sound of her sweet little sigh as I followed her into sleep.

# Chapter 19

WREN

When I woke up, it took me a minute to remember where I was. The rumble of Frank's purr as he lay beside me brought me back with a smile. I still couldn't believe I was in Max's bed. The beauty of that would take some blissful time to get used to.

Max was nowhere to be seen, but I could hear what sounded like breakfast being made in the kitchen. The fact that Max could cook was sexy as hell and very welcome since I certainly couldn't.

I rose from bed gingerly, still sore but feeling better every day. Frank stretched and yawned, giving me an annoyed look for disturbing his slumber as he jumped off the bed and strutted from the room.

I found Max, shirtless and wearing black sweats that hung low on his trim hips, as he stood by the stove, making an omelet. My mouth watered, and it had nothing to do with food.

He turned to watch me approach, his gaze warm, his full lips tipped in a smile. "Hi, baby." He pulled me gently in his arms, and my hands pressed to his firm chest as his lips met mine. I wrapped my arms around his shoulders, deepening the kiss. He growled low, his hands moving to cup my backside covered in only panties and the tee I'd worn to bed.

"You need to wear more clothes if I'm going to control myself," he rumbled against my lips.

"What if I don't want you to control yourself?" I panted as he nipped at my neck, making my knees weak.

He dropped his head to my shoulder. "You're dangerous, woman."

I laughed quietly, holding him against me. "I don't think you have to be quite so careful with me."

His head snapped up at the intention in my words.

I bit my lip, knowing I'd have to convince him a bit. "I want you, Max. Will you touch me? Please?"

He groaned, the sound low and pained. "If only you hadn't said please."

I grinned in triumph as he crouched to slide my panties down my legs before lifting me by the hips onto the counter-top. "That omelet will be ruined, but my breakfast is going to be fucking spectacular." He licked his lips as he lifted my tee carefully over my head.

My heart pounded in anticipation as his mouth dropped to my breast, licking and biting my nipple gently as he continued his journey.

When he reached my core, he looked up at me, biting my inner thigh gently. "You're so fucking gorgeous, Wren," he told me reverently before he took a long, leisurely lick up my center. The sounds of pleasure he made were only eclipsed by my own as I let how good everything he was doing to me be known, loudly.

His tongue explored me eagerly, his large hands gripping my thighs and holding them apart. I was lost to sensation, to his mouth and his fingers as they reached up to tweak my nipples. When his lips zeroed in on my tiny bud of nerves, I nearly came out of my skin. I'd never known anything could feel so good. I also hadn't realized he'd merely been playing until now. Now, he was chasing my orgasm with earnest. When his finger slid inside me, joining the onslaught of pleasure, I lost it, his name escaping my lips and echoing from the rafters as I threw my head back.

He licked me once more before kissing my thighs, my belly, and my breasts, moving up my body with predatory grace.

I wrapped my arms around him, needing him close as I fought for breath, not giving a damn about the twinge in my ribs. He rested his forehead on my shoulder, his arms braced on either side of me, appearing just as moved as I was.

"Can we do that again?" I asked with a grin once I'd collected myself.

He winked. "Every goddamn day."

That suited me just fine.

*       *       *

It was a week later that Max found me in his bedroom digging through my duffle bag for something to wear. "I'm gonna drive you over to your folk's house for a bit," he announced, making my stomach drop.

"So anxious to get rid of me?" I quipped, desperately trying to keep my tone light. I'd been dreading this moment.

We'd spent an amazing week together, reading in his living room, watching movies, and sleeping side by side. He'd started to teach me how to cook, and I was surprised to find I was enjoying it. It had been magic, every day. We were in our own little world, but I knew our cocoon couldn't last forever.

He shook his head. "Just the opposite. I want to make sure you spend some time with your pop. Sal has to know you want to be here, with me. It can't just come from me. I don't think you two have really talked, and you should."

I nodded in agreement, touched by how much he obviously respected my dad. "You're right. We usually talk while we're working on a car together, but we haven't recently because of my injuries."

"I want you to tell him you're going to stay with me."

I turned to face him, my T-shirt clenched in my fist. The idea of having to talk to my dad about that was daunting, but the idea I was misinterpreting Max's words was far worse. "How long are we talking?" I asked cautiously. "Just so I know how much stuff I might need," I added hastily.

"I want you to move in here," he replied calmly, as if he'd just mentioned what we were eating next.

"Move in," I repeated through barely moving lips.

He cocked his head to the side, studying my response. "Do you not want to?"

I sighed. "It's not that. It's just, well, I know you like your space. You're a bit of a loner, Max. A week isn't necessarily a great sample of what it would be like to live with someone else. To live with me," I clarified.

He stepped closer, taking the tee I held and dropping it to the ground. "I like my space better with you in it," he murmured as he dipped to touch my lips with his. "I'm a grown man, babe. I know what I want. I want you. Move in with me, please?"

"If only you hadn't said please." I grinned up at him, throwing his words back at him.

His brows rose expectantly. "That a yes?"

"It's a yes." I grinned, feeling positively giddy with joy.

That joy carried me through our drive passed town toward my parents' house. I missed being on the bike but knew it wouldn't be long now when I could ride with him again.

He dropped me off out front, the engine still running. "I'll be back in a couple of hours."

"If I survive." I groaned dramatically.

He chuckled. "You'll survive. You'd better."

"Love you, babe," I replied, the endearment slipping past my lips as naturally as breathing.

"Love you too." His gaze heated watched me slide down from the truck.

I walked into the house, finding my mom in the living room working on her laptop. "Hi, honey," she greeted with a warm smile. "How are you?"

"Great," I replied sincerely. "I feel a lot better."

"I'm so glad. Did you eat? I have some leftovers in the fridge."

I shook my head. "I'm good." If anything, I was too good in that department. If Max kept feeding me like he had, I'd gain fifty pounds. "Is Pop around?" I asked, trying to sound casual.

She smiled knowingly. "He should be back soon."

I flopped down on the couch next to her, leaning against her like I used to when I was small. She wrapped an arm around me, kissing the side of my head.

"You think he'll be mad?" I whispered. I didn't need to explain what I meant. She knew.

She rested her head on top of mine. "No, honey. He's just..." She sighed. "Sad to let his baby go."

Tears welled in my eyes at the emotion in her words. Clearly my dad wasn't the only one. "I'm not going far. And I was already away at school. That was much farther," I protested lightly.

"This is different." She pressed her lips to my hair. "It's a good different though. You found your man, baby."

"I did." I nodded. "But I'll always need you."

"God, I hope so." She gave a watery laugh. "When you have babies of your own, you'll understand. You want nothing more than to see your child find love, to find someone who will love them with the same selflessness that you do. But at the same time, you fear it because it means you lose a piece of them. Max is the man in your life now, and your father just has to get used to that. And he will. Because he knows Max has that kind of love for you. You are our greatest joy, Wren. From the very first, that's been true."

Tears slid down my cheeks as I burrowed closer to her, and we simply sat, embracing.

"Why are both my girls cryin'?" My dad's demand broke the silence.

We sat up suddenly, my mom laughing as we wiped our cheeks. "Just talking, baby." She assured him with a smile. "How about I make some coffee?" she suggested, standing up. She passed my pop with a tender smile as he hooked her around the waist to kiss her. He never let her walk by without a kiss or some sort of touch.

"You need some help?" I asked him hopefully.

"Sure thing, little bird," he replied with a gentle smile as I followed him out to the garage, a space we'd shared for as long as I could remember.

For a while, we just worked on his car together in silence. Truth be told, there wasn't really all that much left to do on the Chevy, but I had a feeling he wanted the time together as much as I did.

"Would you be up for helping me with the Mustang?" I asked after a while. "Whether or not I can actually drive it is a whole other thing," I added with a grumble.

He chuckled. "Max still tryin' to get you in that Highlander?"

I wrinkled my nose. "Yes, but that isn't happening. I was actually thinking, what if we installed some safety updates to her? Might be considered sacrilege to some, but it feels like a good compromise."

He stood up, wiping his hands with a rag. "That could work. What are you thinking?"

We spent the next hour pouring over research and plans for what we could and couldn't install.

I glanced at my phone, realizing how much time had passed.

"Max comin' back to pick you up?" he asked casually.

I nodded. "He asked me to move in with him," I shared, knowing it was now or never.

There was a pregnant pause before he spoke next. "That what you want?"

"I really do. But it's important to me that you support me. That you support us. I know us getting together wasn't easy on you, but I love him."

He sighed, turning to look at me his blue eyes piercing. "You're my little girl, Wren," his deep voice rumbled. "I think I'll see you that way forever," he admitted. "But you're not. You're an adult, and you have a good head on your shoulders, always have. I admit I didn't handle things well when I first found out about you two. You were easy on me growing up; you never showed much interest in boys. But that means your old man didn't have much practice." He chuckled self-deprecatingly before his expression grew serious. "Max is a good man. He'll take care of you, protect you, and I believe he really loves you. That's about all a father can ask for." He shrugged.

I smiled through tears. "Yeah," I croaked in agreement.

He wrapped an arm around my shoulders. "I'll always be here for you, my little bird. Your mom and I both will. And if he hurts you, I'll kill him."

Many fathers might issue that warning, but with mine, the threat had a very real implication. Despite that, I rolled my eyes, wiping tears from my face for the second time that morning.

"I'll be sure to tell him," I muttered dryly.

"Let's see what we can finish up on these plans before you need to take off." He nodded toward what we'd sketched out. "I'll order these parts, and we can work on it when we get time. She's at the club," he reminded me.

I grinned, relieved that despite so many changes, some of the very best things would be staying the same.

# Chapter 20

"Buy you a beer, sweetheart?" the unfamiliar man on my left asked and was promptly met with a low growl from Max as we sat along the barstools at Mad's.

I rolled my eyes as the man slunk off to a table in the back. "You're such a caveman. It's a good thing you're cute," I scoffed.

"Cute?" he demanded incredulously, clearly not liking that description.

"Cute, hot, and outrageously handsome," I assured him with a grin, leaning into him for a quick kiss.

The past few weeks had been good. Great actually. I'd officially moved in with Max. My injuries were nearly fully healed, and I'd just recently convinced Max to let me ride with him. The summer was nearing its end, and we'd spent a few days at the lake with friends. After a blowup fight, the worst we'd had yet, I'd started back at work with a Knight member always in tow. My nights were spent wrapped up in Max. We'd been taking it slow—well, Max had. If lady blue balls were a thing, I had them.

Max's phone pinged with several texts as I finished my drink. "I'm not gonna be able to take you home tonight," he announced regrettably, looking at me briefly before turning back to his phone to fire off a text.

"What happened?" I asked, trying to hide my concern.

"Nothin' for you to worry about," he was quick to assure me. "But I gotta ride out with a few of the guys tonight. I'll have Gunner take you home and keep an eye on things until I can get there."

I wrinkled my nose at the prospect but knew better than to protest.

He chuckled at my expression. "Hopefully it won't be long. And I'll tell Gun I'll pound him if he's not on his best behavior," he added.

I shot him a skeptical look. It wasn't that Gunner was a bad guy; he just had the sense of humor of a fifth grader.

"I'll be fine," I assured him. I didn't want him worrying about me when, despite his attempts to assure me, I could tell whatever he had to go deal with was important.

He reached over to pull my hand up to his lips, kissing my knuckles before tapping the bar twice and standing up to leave.

I watched him go, hoping the churn in my gut that felt like something terrible was about to happen was wrong for once.

Gunner took me home, striding into the house like he owned it, and after greeting both dogs, moved to the kitchen to immediately forage in the fridge.

"Making yourself comfortable?" I asked with a laugh as he stood up, an apple in his mouth and a beer in hand.

He shrugged. "I'm hungry."

"Want me to make something?" I offered.

"You don't have to," he protested. Obviously, Max's words of warning to be on his best behavior had at least somewhat made their way through.

"It's fine," I assured him, muffling a smile. "How about a grilled cheese?"

His eyes popped comically. "One of my favorites."

I laughed at his enthusiasm. "Okay, I'll get started."

"So, how's being shacked up treatin' you?" he asked, plopping down in one of the barstools and taking a giant bite out of his apple.

I looked at him dubiously. "We're going to small talk, really?"

He chuckled. "Well, damn, Wren, you always did like to bust my balls."

"Wasn't so much something I liked, more something that had to be done." I sighed dramatically.

He shook his head, grinning.

"It's really good," I answered, serious now, looking down at an expectant Sky as she looked up at me, no doubt hoping I'd drop something. "Things with Max, they're good," I shared, waiting for him to tease me.

Instead, he nodded, his gaze sincere. "You two are good together."

"Thanks," I murmured. "How about you?"

"How about me what?"

"Anyone catch your eye around here?" Despite his antics, Gunner had never had a reputation as a ladies' man.

"Nah." He shrugged dismissively.

Something about the way he wouldn't meet my eye said there was more to the story, but I didn't push.

We sat in surprisingly comfortable silence as I finished his sandwich and slid it in front of him.

"It's late. I'm gonna turn in," I told him quietly. "Thanks for staying." As the words left my mouth, the dogs started barking and growling ferociously toward the back patio. I'd never heard them do that, and the hair rose on my neck at the sound.

"Fuck," Gunner bit out, immediately pulling out his phone. "Go lock yourself in the bedroom, back of the closet. Now," he ordered as he held the phone to his ear.

I looked at him wide eyed and turned to do as he asked. Now was not the time to argue, even though despite my fear, I wanted to help. What if he was outnumbered? What if he got hurt? I could hear him on the phone with someone—Max?—telling them to get to the house.

I ran on shaking legs to our bedroom, locking the door behind me. I could hear the dogs, their barking more frenzied as I eyed the bedside table where I knew Max kept a gun. I grabbed it, ready to hide in the closet when the sound of glass shattering from the living room hit my ears at the same time as the bedroom window broke as well.

I stared in horror as a large man climbed in through the window as sounds of a struggle could be heard from the living room.

"Stop right there," I ordered, training the gun on him. Pop had had me shooting at eight years old, and I had damn good aim.

He took a step back, his dark eyes assessing me. He was heavyset with dark beady eyes and a receding hairline. I took him in. He was big but obviously out of shape. Even now he was huffing and puffing from the effort of climbing in through the window. I might not be able to take him, but I could likely outrun him if given the opportunity.

"What do you want?" I demanded.

He sneered. "We're gonna take a little drive," he replied simply.

"I'm not going anywhere with you," I growled, hoping I sounded a lot stronger than I felt.

He took a menacing step toward me.

"Stop," I repeated, holding the gun higher.

He smirked, seeming entirely too comfortable despite my having a gun trained on him.

My heart hammered in my chest as my palms began to sweat.

"Go ahead," he prompted, again taking another step toward me. He didn't think I'd go through with it.

I swallowed hard and pulled the trigger, squeezing my eyes shut.

Nothing happened.

His amused laugh had me opening my eyes in shock. "Looks like you're out of bullets, sweetheart." He smirked, yanking the gun out of my hand.

*Shit.*

# Chapter 21

## MAX

"Somethin's not right," I growled to Maddox as we waited at the drop point along with Cash and Xander. "Are you sure your intel is good?"

Maddox had heard the Rossi's were doing an arms deal inside city limits, and we wanted to be there when it went down. This was our best chance to bring some hurt on those assholes. Now, it was an hour past the time we'd been told, and my instincts were screaming at me to get back to Wren.

"I thought it was, man." Mad shook his head. He had a source he'd used for the past few months, but he wouldn't tell any of us who it was. If I didn't trust the man so damn much, I'd be suspicious. Just as I was going to press him, my phone rang with Gunner's name flashing on the screen.

"Fuck," I swore. "Gun," I barked by way of answer. I knew something had to be way fucking wrong for him to be calling.

"Someone's outside. Need you back here," he replied. I could barely hear him over the sound of the dogs going crazy. "I put Wren in your room, but I don't know how secure that is. Not sure what I'm up against." His tone was calm, but I knew my best friend well enough to detect the underlying stress in his voice.

"We're coming," was all I told him as I hung up and started up my bike. I couldn't spare the time to say more. I didn't need to explain anything to the guys, they'd heard the conversation. Within seconds, our motors were revved and we were hitting the highway back to my house.

Even at the speed I drove, it felt like an eternity to get there. I wasn't accustomed to feeling fear. The thought that something could be happening to Wren in that very moment, that she could be hurt or worse, had me feeling helpless and so fucking angry a red haze had formed in my vision. I had to fight to think clearly through it as I parked off the road a half mile from my house. We needed the element of surprise, and the sound of our bikes wouldn't allow for that.

"Gun didn't say how many," I shared as the guys came to stand alongside me. "I don't know the state of play. We go in quiet."

I didn't wait for agreement but simply took off at a run. I'd never moved so fast in my life. The sound of a gunshot as we neared the house had me doubling my pace.

A glance through the shattered patio doors showed Gunner standing over a dead man, a smoking gun in his hand. "Wren?" I panted, stepping over broken glass.

"In your room. I haven't been back," he replied, his breathing labored. "Was fighting this asshole." He swore, kicking the dead man with his boot.

I ran back to my bedroom, finding both dogs whining at the closed door, the sound making my gut clench in fear. The gnaw and scratch marks proved how hard they'd tried to get into the room. I opened the door and at first didn't understand what I was seeing. The window was shattered, and a large man was laying over Wren. It took me a second to realize he was dead and she was trapped under him.

"Fuck!" I swore, racing into the room, the dogs at my side as I hauled the man off her. Wren crawled into my arms, knocking me to my ass. She was sobbing uncontrollably as I pulled her into my lap, wrapping my arms around her.

"Fucker's dead," Mad announced. "I don't see any wounds." His tone was confused as he and X peered down at the him.

Gunner soon joined us, his face dark with remorse at what he saw. "I'm sorry, Wren. I couldn't get back here." He was shaking his head, clearly tormented. "I had two guys on me. One I took care of. The other ran. Not sure how far he got; Bo got him pretty good," he added, giving Bo an affectionate scratch on the head. "Could have been a lot worse without these two backing me up."

Wren was shaking in my arms, her head buried in my chest. "It's okay, Gun," she managed through chattering teeth. It killed me to see her like this. I wondered how long she'd been trapped under that fat fuck.

His eyes turned to me full of fury. "It was a setup, wasn't it?"

"Must have been," I growled, feeling so stupid for not planning for that possibility and relieved I'd at least thought to have Gunner stay with her.

I'd never make that mistake again.

"What happened?" I asked her quietly as I held her close.

She sniffled and pulled back to look at me with teary eyes. "I came back here when Gunner told me to. I grabbed your gun just as he broke through the window." Her eyes turned to the dead man on the ground. "I tried to shoot him, but the barrel was empty," she whispered.

Another mistake I'd have to correct.

"He thought that was pretty funny." She winced at the memory. "He took it from me, and I don't know, I just sort of attacked him," she admitted. "I knew I didn't have much chance, but it was either that or stand there and let him shoot me."

The idea of my girl trying to take on that hulk of a man was upsetting at best.

"Then he just sort of collapsed," she continued. "I think he had a heart attack or something. Fell right on top of me, and at that angle I couldn't get him off." She shuddered.

Being trapped under a dead man who'd been trying to kill you would scare the shit out of anyone. The fact this had to happen to Wren after everything had me vibrating with rage and regret.

"I'm so fucking sorry," I rasped, holding her to me, not ever wanting to let her go.

She pulled back again to look at me in confusion. "Why would you be sorry?"

I scoffed. "Because I should have kept more men on you. Should have seen this could have been a setup."

She gripped my shoulders. "This is not your fault." Her eyes were bright with determination. "This is no one's fault but theirs."

I squeezed her hips, needing her flesh under my hands. "That gun will always be fully loaded from now on."

She snorted, a small smile tugging at the corner of her mouth. "Or next time I'll just shoot it more than once."

Despite the situation we found ourselves in—in a heap on the ground, glass all around us with a dead man three feet away, my girl managed a smile. If she didn't get how strong she really was, I'd never stop trying to make her see it.

Gunner cleared his throat. "Uh, glad you two are straight and all, but we need to get two dead bodies out of here and figure out what the fuck happened. And I think you might have some repair work to do," he added dryly, his eyes on me.

Wren scooted out of my lap, and I stood, offering her a hand up and pulling her into my side. "Yeah. I'll call Freddy to repair the glass." I nodded. "We can stay at my folk's house tonight," I added, looking down at Wren.

Her eyes were wide and glassy as she nodded.

I shot Gunner a look, one he understood without words.

He nodded once. "Right. I'll ride out over to Cal's. Give him a heads up."

I nodded my gratitude as he left the room.

"Tatum's on his way," Mad put in. "Why don't you take Wren and get out of here? We can take care of this."

"You sure?" I asked. Normally, I'd never even consider it, but with the night Wren had had, I knew I needed to get her out of there.

Mad nodded. "Take care of your girl, Max." He grasped my shoulder briefly before letting go.

"Thanks." I swooped Wren up into my arms, ignoring her shriek of protest as I carried her through the house. "I don't want you stepping on any glass," I told her firmly.

"There's not glass over here!" she exclaimed as I neared the front door, the dogs on my heels.

"Well, maybe I just need to carry you then." It wasn't a lie. Having her weight in my arms helped calm me.

She was silent after that, no doubt sensing I needed this as I deposited her into the passenger side of my truck. The dogs hopped up in the back without hesitation.

"I'll run back inside and get you a change of clothes," I told her. When I went to move away, her fingers held my tee in an iron grip. She looked up at me with wide eyes, telling me without words not to leave her. I leaned into her, pressing my forehead to hers. "Okay, babe. Scratch that idea. We'll just find something of Mom's for you to wear," I murmured, kissing her forehead.

I jogged around the side of my truck, climbing into the driver's seat, and pulled her hand into mine where it would stay until I was forced to let go.

# Chapter 22

## WREN

It was after one in the morning by the time we pulled up in front of Max's parents' house. Despite the hour, both Jill and Cal stood on the front step, Cal's arms wrapped around his wife's shoulders as they watched us approach. Worry shown bright and clear on Jill's face while Cal looked pissed as hell.

I was distantly aware of Cole and Gunner hovering inside, no doubt providing extra security in the event it was needed. It was a terrifying reality that I couldn't even consider at the moment.

Jill didn't try to hug me as she normally would, no doubt sensing how much Max wanted to keep me close. "Your old bedroom is all set up," she murmured to Max. "Mason is home from school for the weekend. He wanted to wait up, but we told him to go to bed," she added, referring to the youngest Jackson.

Max nodded, his arm wrapped around my waist, pulling me in close. "I need to get Wren to bed. We'll talk in the morning," he replied, his eyes on his father.

Cal nodded, watching his son closely. I could tell the wait would be hard for him, but he'd do it for Max.

"Thank you both," I murmured as Max ushered me inside, the dogs right behind us. He guided me upstairs to his old room. It looked much the same as it had when he'd lived here. Though I'd never stepped inside in my years visiting the Jackson home, I'd certainly snuck more than a glance or two during my frequent trips down the hall to Emmie's room.

A double bed lay pushed up against the far wall. A simple desk was against the opposite wall piled with books. A guitar rested in the corner, clearly not one of his favorites since he'd left it here, and motorcycle and music posters covered the walls.

Despite myself, I smiled at the room that reminded me so much of the boy I'd fallen for and the man that was now mine.

Max guided me to sit on the bed, kneeling in front of me. I thought to protest but realized he needed to do this, and frankly, it felt good to be cared for. He examined my feet, reassuring himself I hadn't stepped on any glass. When I expected him to stand, his head dropped into my lap instead, his arms wrapping around my waist.

For a while, we just sat in silence, embracing. I could have said I was fine, but that would have been a lie. Instead, I let him hold me. We both needed it.

Finally, he stood up, pulling me with him. He peeled off my clothes with a focused tenderness that had my heart pounding. He slipped the T-shirt Jill must have left out for me over my head and pulled the covers back. I climbed in dutifully as he shed his own clothes, leaving him in only black boxer briefs.

The sight of his body never failed to make my breathing accelerate.

He climbed in beside me, pulling me into his body and kissing the top of my head.

Despite my exhaustion, I felt too tired to sleep. I propped my chin up on his chest, looking up at him. "I never thought I'd be spending the night in Max Jackson's bedroom." I grinned.

He raised a confused brow. "You spend every night in my bed, babe."

I rolled my eyes. "Yes, but this is *Max Jackson's* bedroom," I emphasized. "The boy I fantasized about for all of middle school and high school. I walked passed it a million times but never dreamed I'd get to sleep in it." I cringed. "I guess that's kind of embarrassing to admit."

He swept my hair back from my face. "More embarrassing than me scaring off any guy who expressed an interest in you? Or going to high school parties just to keep an eye on you?"

His words melted me, but I teased him anyway. "Stalker," I whispered with a grin.

He grinned back, the light moment between us so necessary and reassuring.

"Sleep, baby," he commanded gently.

I nodded against his chest. Despite everything that had happened that night, with my man's arms wrapped around me, his dogs snoring contentedly on the floor beside us, I fell asleep without a second thought.

I woke up alone, stretching stiff limbs as I blearily searched for some clue of the time. I found my phone in my jeans pocket, not surprised that it was after 11:00 a.m. I could hear the sound of pans clanking and the dog's nails on the hardwood downstairs as I pulled my jeans back up my legs.

"Any luck finding the one who got away?" I heard Cal ask as I hit the top of the stairs. I froze midstep, unable to hold off from eavesdropping.

"Not yet," Max grumbled. "We're scouting hospitals. Gunner said Bo got him pretty good."

Cal grunted in approval just as the dogs came bounding up the stairs to greet me, tongues lolling, tails wagging.

"Way to be slick, guys," I whispered, bending to pet them both before making my way downstairs and into the kitchen where every eye turned to me, including Emmie. I wasn't sure when she'd arrived, but I wasn't surprised that she'd come over to make sure both Max and I were all right.

I sided up to Max, feeling slightly shy as I leaned into his side. From what Max had said, both his parents were thrilled Max and I were together, but I was still getting used to the public displays of affection in front of them. He wrapped an arm around me and kissed the top of my head. "Morning, babe. Sleep okay?"

I nodded, eyeing the coffee pot with an enthusiasm that had Jill smiling and busying herself pouring me a cup. It was in her nature to take care of everyone, so instead of fight her on it, I simply smiled and accepted the cup gratefully when she handed it over.

When Mason walked in, wearing sweats and no shirt, I nearly choked on my coffee. He'd put on a ton of muscle since I'd last seen him. I knew he was going to college on a football scholarship. Unlike Cal's other two sons, he hadn't shown an interest in the club. From what Emmie had told me, in true Cal fashion, he'd accepted what his son wanted and supported him 100 percent.

"Go put on a shirt," Max growled irritably.

"What? Why?" Mason demanded, his mouth full of a muffin his mom had baked.

I rolled my eyes at my overprotective man. Mason might be stacked, but Max was the only man I had eyes for.

"Hey, Wren," Mason greeted while trying to dodge Emmie as she tried to grab his food. "Why are you always stealing? Get your own," he complained.

I laughed at their banter, glancing over at Jill, finding her eyes alight with joy. I knew it must mean the world to her to have all three of her kids under one roof.

Cal pulled her in close and kissed her temple before turning his eyes to Max. "You need help at your place today?"

Max shook his head. "It sounds like the guys got the window and patio door boarded up last night."

"Are you guys going to stay here for a while?" Emmie asked.

"You're welcome to," Jill added.

Max was about to respond when I interjected. "That's really thoughtful, but we'll be fine."

Max looked down at me in surprise.

I shrugged. "I want to be at home."

Max kissed the side of my head, pride evident in his expression.

"Plus, Frank is probably already super pissed," I added with a laugh. That cat had more personality than most humans I knew.

"True," Max muttered.

"If you ever change your mind, our door is always open," Jill told us both, reminding me of similar words of welcome she'd bestowed on me many times growing up.

Max slung his arm around my shoulder. "Thanks, Ma. Now, can you pass the muffins before Mason eats all the goddamned food?"

# Chapter 23

## MAX

"Who does that bike belong to?" Wren asked when we pulled up to our house later that morning.

"Cash," I replied. "He texted to say he'd be by to repair the security panel in the master."

She nodded, accepting the gesture of brotherhood without comment. She'd grown up in the club; she knew we had each other's backs, always.

The drone of a drill toward the back of the house sounded, and we headed that way, finding Cash installing a box in the master bedroom. The window was boarded up in there as well, the glass all cleaned up.

Cash's eyes turned to us briefly before returning to work. "Yo. Almost done."

"Thanks, man, appreciate it," I replied meaningfully.

"No worries. By the way, there's cat shit in your tub," Cash shared nonchalantly.

"What!" Wren exclaimed.

"Fucking Frank," I swore, turning to her. "That's his way

of showing us he's pissed we left him."

Her eyes popped wide. "I didn't think cats cared that much about people."

"I don't know about other cats. I just know Frank. And Frank cares," I groused as Cash chuckled at my expense.

"You comin' to the club later to meet on all this shit?" Cash asked, his chin tipped to the broken patio door.

"Yeah," I replied, already planning on taking Wren with me. It'd be a while before I even wanted her in the next room. Last night had shaken me. How close I'd come to losing her, again, wasn't something I'd be getting over anytime soon, if ever.

"I'll come with, work on the car." She shrugged.

It was kind of cute the way she talked about it as though it would have been a choice.

"You want some coffee, Cash?" she offered.

"That'd be great, darlin', thanks," he replied. At my grunt of disapproval over the endearment, he chuckled. "Sorry, let me try again. Thanks, oh sexless one, I would like some coffee."

"Better," I replied as Wren rolled her eyes at me, heading out to the kitchen. I followed her, admiring the sway of her hips as she moved. The minute she reached the kitchen, I tagged her waist, pulling her into me.

I took her mouth, getting hard instantly at having her close. I needed inside her. These last few weeks exploring her, learning every curve had been incredible, but I needed all of her.

As if sensing my train of thought, she pulled back, looking up at me with her eyes glazed by lust. She was ready to give herself to me. And I was ready to take.

"Later." I nipped her lower lip, grabbing the globes of her ass in my hands.

"Later," she agreed breathlessly, knowing exactly what I meant.

Later couldn't come soon enough.

\*    \*    \*

*Got a present for you*

Mad's text had my interest piqued as Wren and I got ready to leave the house.

*Be there in 20*

I started up the bike as Wren swung up behind me. I loved having her on the back of my bike. I pulled her arms around me tight as we made our way down the drive, Cash following behind us.

When I walked in the clubhouse, there were a couple of prospects milling around along with a few cherries. After making sure Wren was straight in the garage, I headed down the hall toward the doors where only patched members were welcome.

I found Mad, Gunner, and X standing over an unfamiliar man slumped in the lone chair that stood in the middle of the room.

"Told you I had a gift." Maddox looked up at me with a wicked grin.

"Who's this?" I asked in confusion.

"We've been canvassing hospitals within 100 miles of here. Guess who turned up with an infected bite wound?" X shared before glowering down at the groaning man. "You should have let that shit fester, asshole," he taunted, delivering a swift kick to the chair.

Understanding dawned as I stepped further into the room, shutting the door behind me. This was the asshole who got away. Finding him was a stroke of luck, and we all knew it.

"Figured this might make up for my bad intel," Mad grumbled.

"I still want to talk about that," I warned before turning my eyes to the hunched figure. "My dog got a good taste of you, huh?" I snickered, my gaze on the man's bandaged leg.

"Those dogs are fucking crazy!" he grunted in pain.

"When someone comes in and threatens their home and their mistress, then fuck yes, they are," I replied with pride. "Now, let me tell you how this is gonna go. You're gonna tell us what we want to know, and maybe, just maybe, the dog bite will be the worst of your injuries. Let's start with your name."

The guy whimpered, clearly terrified, which led me to believe he wasn't a career criminal. He didn't look that old, maybe twenty. We could use all of that to our advantage. "Johnny," he answered finally.

"Johnny...?" Cash kicked his chair.

"Johnny Mann," he replied quietly.

The name didn't mean anything to me. "Who gave the order to attack my house?" I demanded.

"I don't know his name," he replied, receiving a threatening growl from Xander.

"I don't!" he sputtered. "I was working with my cousins. They had more direct contact."

"What did he want?" I demanded.

"He... he wanted the girl," he blathered. "He said he'd set up a distraction so we could go in and take her."

That explained the false intel.

"We were supposed to grab her and take her to an address in Reno. Then we'd get the money."

My pulse pounded with rage. "What did he want with her?"

"I don't know." He shook his head. "I never talked to him directly, but it sounded like he was an ex-boyfriend or something. That he wanted her back."

Realization slammed into me. "Her fucking stalker," I growled low to Gunner who nodded solemnly.

Johnny looked at me with fear-filled eyes. "Are you going to kill me?"

"We might," X broke in. He always loved this kind of shit.

"Not if you're useful." I shot a pointed look at X to shut it. "You find me someone who talked to that piece of shit directly and give me the address you were supposed to take the girl to," I said, not wanting to use Wren's name. "And maybe we'll let you live."

"I can try." He nodded frantically.

X had him by the throat so fast I barely saw him move. "You'll do more than fucking try."

X let him go, leaving Johnny to cough and sputter for breath. "I can get you the address, but you already killed my cousins who knew everything," he protested.

Fuck. He had a point.

"Technically, one died on us, literally," Cash put in dryly.

I paced the room, ignoring Cash. How did Wren's stalker know about our business with the Rossi's? Obviously, he knew enough to set us up so we'd be away from my place. And he was obviously getting desperate to pay kidnappers to make such a bold attempt at a snatch and grab.

"Get what else you can out of him," I grunted to X. "I need to get back to Wren." Even knowing she was safe inside club walls, she was still too far from me.

X offered a chin lift as I strode out of the room, trying to get a handle on the fear and fury equally permeating through my system.

This needed to end, and soon. I'd never looked forward to having blood on my hands so much in my life.

# Chapter 24

WREN

I'd just slammed the hood shut on the Mustang, content with what I'd done for the day, when Max walked into the garage. He didn't pause when he saw me, but instead walked directly into my space, pulling me against him and taking my mouth with a kiss so intense all I could do was cling to him for support and give myself over to his mouth.

"We're going now," he panted against my mouth.

My entire body shivered at his throaty command as he tagged my hand and began to pull me toward his bike.

My laughter at his haste was promptly swallowed when he pressed me up on the nearest wall, his expression nearly feral. "I have a very loose hold on my control," he warned. "So, let me tell you what's gonna happen. I'm gonna get us home, and you're going to take that fine ass in the house and strip for me. I want you on the bed, and I don't want anything hiding that body from me. Can you do that?"

Instead of feeling shy as I would have just mere weeks ago, I was unbelievably turned on by his request and nodded dutifully.

"Good girl," he murmured, his eyes straying to my lips before he backed off, pulling me once again toward his bike.

My heart hammered in my chest as we hit the freeway, anticipation like a living thing between us. Surprisingly, I wasn't nervous. Not with Max. Instead, all I felt was exhilaration that the man I'd coveted for years was about to be mine.

"Remember what I said," he reminded me, his voice an octave lower than normal, after we pulled up in front of his house.

I bit my lip and nodded. Getting off the bike, I headed for the house. I dismantled the alarm the way Max had showed me and walked on shaking legs back to the bedroom.

I rid myself of my clothing, my hands trembling as I unhooked my bra and slid my panties down my legs. I crawled onto the bed as ordered, my heart hammering in my chest as I waited for Max. I didn't need to wait long. Within moments he appeared in the doorway, his dark eyes sweeping over me.

"Christ, you're perfect," he breathed reverently, his tongue licking his bottom lip in anticipation.

He truly believed that, I knew he did.

"I don't know where to start," he admitted hungrily.

I squirmed on the bed. "Well, you'd better start somewhere," I warned, "or I'm going to have to take care of things myself."

His brows rose. "Is that right? That I have to see, but not yet. Not today. Today, you're all mine." He pulled his tee off with one hand, revealing the gorgeous abs I'd kissed at every opportunity. His pants came next, leaving him in boxer briefs that did nothing to conceal just how much he wanted me.

He crawled up from the bottom of the bed, kissing me as he went. When he came to my core, he breathed in deep as though my scent gave him life. His journey continued, licking my belly button before ravishing each breast with his lips and tongue. By the time he reached my mouth, I was a bundle of frantic desire.

He settled between my legs, pressing against me deliciously as he took my mouth. There was nothing frantic about his movements. His kiss was deep and leisurely, as though he had all the time in the world.

My hands caressed the glorious muscle in his arms before raking over his broad back in a bid to somehow contain what was already building inside me.

He took up a slow rhythm, pressing against me as his teeth nipped at my neck and shoulder. I'd never known that a small bite of pain turned me on that much more. Max had discovered that and had frequently used it to his advantage to drive me absolutely crazy.

"Take these off," I panted, my fingers at the hem of his boxers.

"Soon," he promised, chuckling at my groan of frustration. "There's only one first time with you," he murmured, dropping a kiss on my collarbone.

"There will also be a second and a third," I reminded him on a moan as his fingers danced over the bundle of nerves screaming for attention.

"And a twentieth and a hundredth," he interjected, not pausing his ministrations. "I told you I'd be your first and last, and I meant it."

I cupped his face in my hands, staring up at the man I'd fallen in love with so absolutely that there was no question he was my forever. "I know." My breath hitched as a light sheen of sweat broke out over my skin. He played my body like an instrument, watching with hooded eyes as he brought me over the edge.

"You're so beautiful," he murmured as I shuddered in his arms. Finally, when I'd managed to control my breathing somewhat, he moved away from me, but only so far as to slip off his boxers.

"It's gonna hurt this first time, babe. Then, it'll be so fucking good. Promise." He swore as he moved in between my legs, pressing against my entrance.

I bit my lip and nodded, forcing myself to relax as he nudged inside me.

It stung as he pushed further. I was small, and Max definitely was not. But it was a good kind of pain because it meant I was as close to him as you could be with another person.

"Christ, you feel so good. Are you okay?" he managed through gritted teeth.

I nodded as he pressed all the way inside me in one fluid thrust. He paused, giving me a moment to adjust. He was being so careful with me, I knew it took everything in him to take me slow.

"I'm okay, Max. I need you to move." I marveled at the full feeling of having him inside me.

He picked up his rhythm to a slow and steady tempo that had me gasping for breath. His fingers moved between my legs, eclipsing the bite of pain with pleasure as he brought me with him toward the pinnacle.

When he bit down on my shoulder, I cried out his name, hurdling over the edge with him immediately behind me.

He groaned out my name, the throaty rumble the most beautiful sound. He collapsed gently on top of me, licking at the small mark he'd created as I wrapped my arms and legs around him, wanting to keep him inside me just a bit longer despite the pain.

He kissed my neck before lifting his head to look me in the eye. "I love you, Wren."

"I love you too," I replied, feeling so deliciously full both body and soul.

He slid out of me gently, watching my face the entire time. I gave him a smile, assuring him I was okay. "Let's take a bath." He pulled me up off the bed and toward the bathroom. "It'll help with the soreness."

I would have rather stayed in bed, but I could tell he needed to take care of me, so I nodded and followed him into the bathroom.

Once we slipped into the bubbles, I leaned back against his chest with a pleasure-filled moan. He'd been right. The warm water immediately reduced the ache between my legs.

He wrapped his arms around me, kissing my jaw as we lay in comfortable silence. I took his large hand in mine, tracing over the rough patches earned from working on his bike and lifting weights to the soft patch on the top of his hand, never having felt so content.

"Did you find out anything?" I asked quietly.

His body noticeably stiffened under mine. "Let's talk about it later."

"Bu—" I started to protest.

He squeezed me, gently kissing my neck. "I'll tell you what I know but later. Right now, I want to hold your sexy-as-fuck, soapy little body against mine and hope the bath soothes you enough so I can take you again and then make you some dinner."

I barely suppressed a moan and decided I could wait to find out any details he'd learned. Tonight was about Max and me.

# Chapter 25

## MAX

I sipped coffee on the back deck the next morning, staring out over the landscape as the sun rose above the mountains to the east. I'd needed to get out of bed—it was too tempting to take Wren again, and I knew she was sore.

Last night had been one of the best of my life. She'd given herself to me so willingly. Nothing better.

I watched the dogs sniffing their way through their territory, ever watchful as Frank hopefully unsuccessfully hunted for mice.

The door slid open behind me, and I turned to watch Wren step toward me dressed in nothing but one of my tees and panties.

I pulled her into my side, grabbing her ass as I took her mouth in what I'd intended to be a soft kiss but quickly turned out to be much more.

"You weren't in bed," she accused when we finally broke apart, her lips swollen and pink.

"You're sore, and if I'd stayed, I don't think I could have helped myself," I admitted ruefully.

She smiled, clearly pleased. "What's on for today?"

I shrugged. "Was hoping we could take it easy. There's a thing at the club tonight, but we can go only if we feel like it."

"That sounds great," she agreed. "What are those brochures on the counter?"

"Kevin dropped by some patio door design ideas yesterday. I was waiting for you to have a look at them."

"Me? Why?"

"So I don't pick something you don't like," I replied, as though it should be obvious, and it should be.

"Max, it's your house." She still sounded utterly confused.

"No." I shook my head slowly, calling for patience. "It's *our* house. It became your house when you moved in, before that even." I stepped closer to her cupping her jaw in my hands, tipping her face up to look at me. "Figured you'd know that since you let me inside you last night, since I'm the only man that has ever been there or will ever be there, and since you love me and I love the fuck out of you, that you're mine in every sense of the word."

I watched the pulse kick in her neck as a gorgeous blush tinged her cheeks.

"If you don't like it here, then we can find a different place, but gotta tell you, babe, I like the space and the quiet."

"I love it here too, Max."

"So, you get me?" I prompted with a swat to her backside.

"I get you," she replied with a gorgeous smile.

I grinned, knowing I smiled so much more often now that she was in my life. "Great. Now, will you please go pick some doors? I hate doing that shit," I grumbled.

"Bossy," she muttered without ire.

"Your cross to bear, sweetheart."

\* \* \*

When we walked into the club later that night, hand in hand, Wren was almost immediately pulled away by Ginnie, X's woman, chattering something about the salon.

With her purple hair and sleeve of tattoos, Ginnie had never been afraid to stand out or to speak up. She and X were perfect together.

I watched Wren go, eyeing her delicious ass I'd sunk my teeth in the night before, the memory the only perk of her walking away from me.

"Max, wasn't sure you'd make it out," X goaded as he handed me a beer.

"A warm, soft woman or you assholes? It was a tough choice." I snorted.

He grinned, clinking his beer with mine. "I know exactly what you mean," he replied, his eyes on Ginnie.

"Mad around?" I asked, surveying the room packed with club members, old ladies, and a few cherries.

"Out back. Scar made her ribs, so I was just headed that way." X tilted his head toward the back patio where a fire pit was lit and the barbeque was getting a workout. Cole's wife, Scarlet, made the best damn ribs I'd ever had. But that wasn't what I was focused on tonight.

That source of Mad's had been bothering me ever since the attack at my house. I wanted to know who it was to make sure we didn't get caught with our pants down again.

"There aren't many left," Maddox said by way of greeting as he mowed through the last rib on his plate.

"I'm good," I declined. "I wanted to talk to you."

Sensing my mood, he stood up straighter, dropping the rib on his plate. "What about?"

"Your source," I replied. "Bad information almost got my woman snatched. I want to know who it is."

He cocked his head to the side, his gray eyes assessing me. "No."

"No?" I demanded as X and Gunner joined our tense discussion.

"What's going on?" Gun asked.

"I want to know who Mad's source is," I told him.

Mad sighed, running a hand over his whiskers. "Listen, I understand why you'd be pissed." He was clearly trying to diffuse the situation. "But that information? It had nothing to do with my source. She was fed wrong information herself."

"It's a she?" I demanded, incredulously.

Maddox winced. Clearly, he hadn't meant to share that piece of information. "Fuck. Yes, it's a she," he acknowledged. "And she's risking her ass telling me anything. All her intel up until now has been good. I promised I'd protect her identity, even from you, and I intend to keep that promise."

I cocked my head to the side, studying my friend. "You have feelings for this woman?"

He looked torn as to how to respond. "It's complicated."

"Isn't it always?" Gunner snorted.

Mad eyed me steadily. "My feelings have nothing to do with her intentions, which I know are pure. I trust her, Max. I need you to take my word on it. I'm not telling you who she is."

"Fine," I agreed after a pause. The truth was, I trusted Maddox implicitly. Though that wouldn't stop me from digging deeper the next time we got intel.

"Thank you," he replied seriously.

"Phew, now that's over, let's have a fucking drink, yeah?" Gunner chortled, always the first to try to lighten the mood.

"Yeah," I agreed as Wren slipped under my arm. Instantly, my mood lightened. "Hi, babe. What are you girls up to?"

"Not much. I'm going to spend part of the morning at the salon with Ginnie and Grace tomorrow," she shared as Ginnie sidled up to X, and he promptly pulled her in close.

I looked at my girl, not eager to have anything change about her appearance. "What are you doing at the salon?"

"Don't worry. You'll like whatever we do." Ginnie tried to reassure me with a wink.

"You don't need to change anything. You're perfect," I mumbled grumpily.

Wren laughed a bit uncomfortably. "I'm glad you think so."

I knew so but sensed I'd embarrass her if I pressed the subject. "We'll need to get a man on you. I have shit to do for a few hours in the morning, but I can take over in the after-noon."

"I can do it," X offered. I wasn't surprised; it would give him an excuse to be close to Ginnie, even if that meant hanging around the salon.

"Okay, well now that the babysitters are lined up, we can live our lives," Wren mumbled.

I kissed her temple. "It's temporary, babe. Not that I won't always want to follow you around," I added.

I was only partially kidding.

"I know." She sighed. "I just hate feeling like a burden."

"It's not a problem," X was quick to assure her, and I shot him a grateful look. "I need to get my tips frosted anyway," he added, pointing to his bald head.

Ginnie rolled her eyes with a grin. "Yeah, babe. While we're at it, we'll get in that time machine and go back to when that was actually cool."

"And to when you had hair," Cash put in with a grin.

"Fuck off," X rumbled without malice, grabbing the last of the ribs, the ultimate revenge.

# Chapter 26

"You look hot," Gracie assured me the next morning as she blew out my hair after a cut that had left me with badass layers and sideswept bangs.

"I love it." I beamed at her. Grace was hell on wheels with scissors. I was proud of my friend and all too happy to reap the benefits.

The salon was beautiful, with a sleek modern design and top-of-the-line products.

"We should go out tonight!" she exclaimed, looking over at Ginnie who was cutting hair at the station to the right.

"We totally should," Ginnie agreed readily.

"I'm not sure Max will be cool with that," I hedged, fretting. "He's been in super vigilance mode." I grimaced, knowing it was warranted given the danger I was in.

"We'll get a bunch of the guys on board," Grace suggested. "Will you let me dress you?" she added hopefully.

"She's not a Barbie doll, Grace." Ginnie snorted.

"Oh fine," I huffed as Gracie pouted. It was so hard to

say no to her. Whatever man claimed her was seriously fucked.

She gave a little hop of excitement. "We'll get ready at my place. I'll text Em."

I nodded, knowing it was out of my hands at this point and not really minding.

"We'll have to make sure Mr. Clean can come with," Grace added, her gaze on Xavier who had crammed his huge body into one of the chairs at reception. He was hunched over reading a tattoo magazine and looked the opposite of comfortable.

"Hey, lady, don't make fun of my man," Ginnie warned. "That's my right and my right only."

Gracie laughed and nodded her agreement as she continued to contort my hair into all kind of loops with the brush in her hand. She'd given me a tutorial, but I knew I'd never recreate what she'd done.

"Voila." She beamed a few minutes later when she finished putting a bit of product in. I stared at myself in the mirror, shaking my head back and forth, reveling in the lighter feel. She'd taken off several inches, though my hair still hung well past my shoulders. The layers added a dimension I hadn't had before, and the bangs made my eyes pop.

"You're awesome, Grace," I complimented. "Seriously."

"Thanks." She grinned, clearly pleased with her work. "Do you want to head over to my place? I'm off in a couple of hours but Emmie's home already. We can watch movies and hang out until it's time to get ready."

"Sounds fun," I agreed as I slid out of the chair. Max had texted to tell me he was tied up for the day. Plus, some time with my girls sounded perfect. I'd missed them. "When are you off, Gin?"

"Not till tonight. I'll either meet you guys at Grace's or meet you out," she answered.

"Sounds good. I'll see you both soon." I waved as I practically bounced over to the changing room where I shucked my robe and slid my tee shirt back over my head.

"All set?" X asked when I emerged. He stood up stiffly and stretched. "Fuck those chairs are small."

"Or you're just big," I pointed out with a smile. "I was going to head over to Em and Gracie's place. Max is busy. That okay by you?"

"Sure." He nodded easily. "I'll follow you over there. I bet Gunner can take over for me for a few hours."

I cocked my head to the side. "Why, because I'll be at Em's?"

He looked uncomfortable for a moment before shrugging. "I think he's just around today," he answered vaguely.

Yeah, sure. Someday I'd get to the bottom of what was between those two.

∗　∗　∗

"Max is going to lose his marbles," Emmie announced later that night as Grace guided me in front of the floor-length mirror in her bedroom where we'd spent the day binge watching TV, eating pizza, and being lazy.

Their two-bedroom bungalow was cozy with it's hardwood floors, warm-toned paint, and comfortable furniture. It was definitely a home where women lived, but not overly girly.

"He so is." Grace beamed, looking over my shoulder.

I bit my lip nervously as I stared at my reflection. Grace had dressed me in a formfitting black halter shirt tucked into skinny, high-waisted, black jeans. She'd finished the look with open-toes booties that Ginnie had insisted on once she'd joined us. For most, this wouldn't be considered sexy, but for me, it was definitely a step outside my comfort zone.

"I held myself back a bit knowing you wouldn't want to go beyond this," Grace explained. "But, Wren, you look beautiful. You have an absolutely gorgeous figure." She grinned. "Trust me."

"Seriously, girl." Ginnie nodded in agreement.

"Okay," I murmured, still slightly unsure but trusting that they wouldn't steer me wrong.

"Next time, we'll show some cleavage, but this is a start." Grace winked.

"Right," I muttered.

"So how do we look?" Ginnie asked Gunner when we emerged into the living room where he was sitting staring at his phone.

He looked up at her briefly. "I like my head connected to my body, so I'm not saying shit."

Ginnie rolled her eyes. "X won't care if you say we look nice, Gun."

He snorted. "Have you met your man? Have you met hers?" he demanded, pointing at me. No thanks." He shook his head.

"Well okay, how about Em?" Grace prompted, pointing at Emmie who was wearing a skirt that showed off her gorgeous legs and a black top that showed a hint of midriff.

His dark eyes lifted to Em, holding briefly. For a moment, the tension was so thick between them I could swear the spark sizzled in the room. "Too much skin," he mumbled finally.

I wanted to groan my frustration at the lost opportunity.

Emmie looked down, a flash of hurt in her gaze before she immediately masked it with a look of annoyance. "Let's go," she mumbled.

I shot a glare at Gunner as I followed my friend out the door. The four of us piled into Ginnie's Honda, with Em and Grace in the back seat, while Gunner fired up his bike behind us.

"You look hot, Em," I assured her once we'd pulled away from the curb. "And Gun thinks so," I added meaningfully.

"Definitely," Ginnie agreed.

"I don't care what that idiot thinks," Em grumbled.

Grace turned to look at her with a raised brow, silently challenging her. "It's obvious there's something going on between you," she pointed out gently. "I don't get why you both fight it so hard."

"There's nothing going on between us," she sputtered.

"There would be if you'd both stop being so stubborn," Grace shot back.

"Yaaas, girl!" Ginnie exclaimed with exuberant support.

"You both suck." Emmie pouted as Ginnie cranked the stereo, filling the car with her standard classic rock.

When we pulled up in front of Mad's, the only bar the guys would approve of us going to, the mood in the car was decidedly lighter.

Gunner followed us inside, taking up residence at the bar while the four of us found a table.

"So how long you think until our men make an appearance?" Ginnie asked with a lifted brow toward me as we sipped our first round.

The idea was for this to be a girls' night, but I doubted we'd be alone for long. "An hour?" I laughed.

"I give it thirty minutes," she replied, not looking annoyed in the slightest. She and X had been together for years, and I loved how protective he still was of her and how much they clearly enjoyed being together.

I could only hope Max and I felt the same in the years to come. Somehow, I knew instinctively that we would.

I got up to use the restroom after we'd ordered another round of drinks.

"Darlin', you're just about the prettiest sight I've ever seen," a southern drawl sounded behind me.

I turned to face the unfamiliar biker, planning to offer a swift rejection, more for his sake than mine. He stepped closer, licking his lips.

"You take one step closer to my woman, Booker, and we're gonna have a problem." Max's snarl sounded as he appeared behind the man who he obviously knew.

The man raised his hands. "Sorry, Jackson. I didn't realize she was spoken for. No harm done." He shook his head, backing away immediately.

I took a deep breath, relieved that the brief confrontation was over quickly. "Thank you for not acting like a cavema —" My words were abruptly cut off as Max took my mouth in a punishing kiss while walking us toward the bathroom, shoving the door open and locking it behind us.

"You look... you look... why do you look like this?" he

panted, seeming at a loss for words as he pressed me up against the door.

"Do you not like it?" I asked worriedly.

"You look amazing, babe. I love it. What I don't like is that you were out without me looking like this."

"It's jeans and a blouse, honey." I laughed at his overprotectiveness while inwardly reveling in it at the same time.

"The way you wear it, it might as well be lingerie," he growled, unzipping my jeans to slide his hands down to my backside, squeezing firmly.

"What are you doing?" I gasped as his finger slipped inside me from behind.

He took my mouth again by way of answer, his tongue moving in time with his finger. Then he was on his knees and shoving my pants down my legs. His mouth was on me before I could utter a word of protest, not that I would have just then.

My head slammed back against the door as I fought the urge to moan loud enough for the entire bar to hear.

His tongue was beautiful torture, moving over me expertly as his lips joined the onslaught. In record time, I was gasping his name, my legs shaking, my entire body suffused with heat as I rode out my orgasm.

He stood up slowly, his hands caressing my legs and hips as he went. He kissed me again, achingly slow. "I like the hair too," he murmured against my mouth.

I grinned just as a knock sounded on the door. "Oh my God!" I whispered, blushing profusely.

He grinned wickedly, leaning down to help me with my jeans. "One look at you, no one would blame me." He shrugged unperturbed by the interruption or the fact it was obvious what we were doing.

Once my clothes were squared away, he took my hand, unlocking the door and leading me out into the hall. "Ladies," he greeted the women waiting in line with an easy smile.

They looked back at him with wide eyes, stunned into silence. If I had to guess, they were more befuddled by my gorgeous man than what we'd been doing.

I looked down, biting back a smile as he led me back to our table. One thing was for sure, life with Max would never be dull.

# Chapter 27

## MAX

Later that night, I lay in bed with Wren in my arms. I'd taken her twice after we'd gotten home, still feeling the need to claim her, to mark her. The taste I'd had in the bathroom earlier hadn't been nearly enough.

"You have fun tonight?" I asked, burrowing my face into her neck.

"Yeah." She yawned.

"I wear you out?" I grinned playfully.

"You know you did." Her satisfied smile was sexy as hell.

"You looked beautiful tonight," I told her again. "But you're just as gorgeous in jeans and a tee with grease all over you," I added honestly. That was the girl I'd fallen in love with.

"Thanks." She smiled. "It felt good. I just needed the push that Gracie and Em are always willing to provide. If they have anything to say about it, there's a shopping spree coming up in my very near future."

I snorted, knowing that was all too true. My sister never turned down the opportunity to shop or to provide a nudge, or a shove when needed. "Don't let those two have you showing too much skin," I warned.

"I won't," she murmured drowsily, dropping her head back to my chest. I sensed she was just moments from falling asleep. "What's the deal with Emmie and Gunner?" she asked, almost as an afterthought.

I tensed, surprised by the question. "What do you mean?"

"Have you told him he can't date her or something?"

"No. Does he want to date her?" I asked in shock. The idea I might be missing the fact that my best friend had feelings for my little sister was disconcerting.

"You've never noticed the tension between them?"

"No." In fact, I spent energy trying *not* to pay attention to my sister's love life.

I felt her shrug against me. "Well, who knows what it is. Both of them are stubborn as hell about it." She looked up at me with wide eyes. "Don't tell either of them I said anything."

I looked back at her with a wrinkled brow. "Babe, based on this conversation, I'm not even sure what the hell we're talking about here."

She relaxed and rolled her eyes. "You're such a guy."

"Hope I don't need to prove that you again," I replied dryly.

She let out a tired laugh. "You can prove it to me again tomorrow. How about that?"

I pulled her closer, kissing the top of her head. "Sleep, babe."

"Love you, Max."

I'd never tire of hearing those words. "Love you too, baby."

\*   \*   \*

I stood under the showerhead the next morning, smiling to myself at the thought of Wren in the kitchen making breakfast. Food had been the farthest thing from my mind when I'd woken with her long-ass legs tangled with mine, but she was on a mission. I'd been teaching her how to cook, and little by little, she was getting the hang of it. We'd started simple, but she was eager and so fucking cute. We'd ended up on the kitchen floor more times than with a finished meal, but it had been a hell of a lot of fun.

I thought about the ring I'd bought for her. It sat in my bedside table drawer just itching to be on her finger. I'd bought it weeks ago, but I wanted Sal's blessing, and I wanted this shit with her stalker done with. I wanted us to start our life together free and clear, without a hint of the fear I saw clouding her gorgeous eyes when she thought I wasn't looking.

X was staying on top of Johnny and seemed to think he was doing what he could to run down an address for us in Reno. It would be a start—a start that would lead us to the end of this fucking mess.

When I heard the doorbell clang, I hastily threw on my shirt, wondering who would show up here without letting me know ahead of time. Everyone knew how on edge I was when it came to Wren.

I stalked out to the living room, tensing when I saw she had the door open to someone. Her expression immediately had me on edge. "What is it?" I demanded a moment before I spotted the woman on the other side.

All the air left my lungs, and for the first time since I could remember, my legs wobbled beneath me.

"This woman says she's your mother," Wren murmured, her eyes full of concern. She knew Jill wasn't my birth mother, but beyond that, she didn't know much. I kept that information locked down tight, always had.

"Hi, Max," my birth mother, Janelle, greeted quietly.

My memories of her from childhood were cloudy, but I could assess that she looked much older than she should, years in prison would do that to anyone. She also appeared to be sober, which was not something I'd seen a lot as a kid.

I moved to stand beside Wren, glaring at the hauntingly familiar woman on the other side of the door. "What the fuck are you doing here, Janelle?" I demanded once I'd found my voice. I'd never expected to see her again after she'd abandoned Emmie and me at a motel over twenty years ago. We could have died had I not been able to reach Jill. She and Cal had taken us home that very night, and we'd never looked back. I'd never wanted to, and yet, here was my ugly past staring me right in the face.

"I just got out," she admitted. "I wanted to see you and your sister."

The possibility of her even setting eyes on Emmie enraged me. "You mean you want to see the daughter you abandoned when she was four years old?" I thundered. "You want to see the kids you tried to have kidnapped once we were finally living clean?"

She flinched at my rage, and I watched without pity as she fought for composure. "I was a mess back then, I know," she acknowledged. "I'm trying to get my life back together."

"Well, do it without me and Emmie. If I hear that you even breathed the same air as her, I'll make sure you end up back behind bars where you belong," I snarled.

"Max, please," she whispered, her eyes full of tears.

"No." I shook my head. "You don't get a second chance. Hell, it wouldn't even be a second chance or a third or fourth. You had plenty of those already. You made a choice. You chose to shoot shit up your veins rather than care for us. You made a choice to fucking abandon us in a motel by the side of the highway that most guests paid for by the hour. Get the fuck out. I don't ever want to see you again."

She nodded once through tears. "I thought you might respond this way. I'm staying at the Hampton Inn if you change your mind and want to talk."

"Not gonna happen," I bit out, watching as she pulled her purse further up her shoulder and, with a sad smile at Wren, made her way back to her car.

My chest heaved as I stared after her, hating feeling weak even for a moment. When Wren's hand pressed gently to my back, I flinched away from her touch. I was too raw and too angry to face her now.

"Max—"

"Don't." I shook my head. "I know what you're gonna say. That I was too harsh. That I should have talked to her."

"That's not what I was going to say at all," she countered. "Don't shut me out, babe. I'm on your side."

I snorted, unable to quell the fury welling up inside me. "Save the hallmark bullshit, all right, Wren?"

She reeled back from my words. "Don't try to hurt me because you're hurting, Max," she ordered, fire lighting her gorgeous eyes.

I needed to get away—from the look in her eyes, from the house, hell, from this town all together.

"You haven't shared much about her," she noted quietly. "But from everything you said, she doesn't deserve you or Emmie. Don't be ashamed. She's no reflection on you."

The fact that she'd zeroed in so precisely on what I was feeling—shame—pissed me right the hell off. I wouldn't be weak. Not because of that poor excuse for a mother.

"I don't feel anything other than pissed," I barked, unable to quell my temper.

She flinched at my tone.

Fuck, I couldn't seem to stop myself from lashing out.

"You don't talk about her," she noted softly.

"I don't think about her, ever," I snapped.

Her eyes filled with unshed tears. "Yeah, clearly you have no issues, Max," she shot back hoarsely.

I sucked in a breath, trying like hell to calm down. "Look, I need to get out of here for a while."

She crossed her arms over her chest, the defensive gesture that I'd created, twisting my already churning insides to the point of pain. She watched me stoically, unmoving as I gathered my jacket and keys.

"Max, what are you doing?" she demanded quietly, her gaze seeing right through my anger to the pain underneath. She'd always been able to read me, and right now, I couldn't stand having her see me laid bare.

"I'll get Gunner over here in five minutes. Lock the door, set the alarm," I ordered by way of answer.

The shit of it was, I just couldn't seem to stop myself from running. And that's exactly what I was doing. It was as though the memory of Janelle was cloying at my insides, making me itch. Making me ache.

I tore away from the house, kicking up gravel as I went trying to escape my past and knowing I could very well be fucking up my future.

# *Chapter 28*

I lay staring up at Emmie and Grace's ceiling that night, feeling a mixture of worry over Max, who I still hadn't heard from, and anger at him for how he'd treated me. I thought I'd had him, all of him. But as it turned out, he'd been holding himself back this entire time, and that hurt a whole hell of a lot worse than anything he'd said in anger. There was part of him I'd never touched, a piece of him that he held back from everyone, including me. Was that love?

When Emmie appeared with a cozy blanket in tow, I watched her mutely as she walked into the kitchen, grabbed something from the refrigerator, and sat on the couch, moving my legs into her lap. She produced a pint of ice cream and two spoons.

"Who needs dinner when we can have ice cream?" She shot me a warm smile before her expression grew pensive. "Have you heard from him?"

I shook my head. "I know it's only been a few hours, but he's never done anything like this before. Part of me is worried, and the other is so freaking mad at him I can't even think straight."

She nodded. "He deserves it. He shouldn't have left the way he did."

"Are you okay?" I asked, feeling like a heel for not asking sooner. "With Janelle being out?" Both Max and Emmie seemed to prefer to refer to their birth mother by name, so I followed their lead.

She shrugged, swallowing a bite of ice cream. "Yeah. I really am. I was younger than Max. I don't even really remember her. Jill has always been my mom as far as I'm concerned. And what negative memories I would have had, Max always protected me from."

"He's a good big brother," I murmured.

"The very best."

"He's never talked about her with me."

"He's never talked about it with anyone that I know of." She handed over the ice cream. "I don't know how much he's really thought about it. Max can be hard to read. One thing I do know for sure," she continued firmly, "is that my brother loves you."

It was the first time I'd doubted it, and just when I needed to believe it the most.

When a knock sounded on the front door, we both turned in surprise. X was posted out front, so whoever it was didn't pose a threat.

Emmie rose and headed for the door. "What are you two doing here?" she asked Gunner and Cash as they stepped into the room.

"We wanted to check on Wren," Cash returned, his blue eyes landing on me.

I bit back a smile, my heart warming at the knowledge

that these guys weren't just Max's friends anymore. They were mine too.

"I'm okay," I assured them just as I noticed Gunner's jacket was wriggling.

"Do you have a dancing tumor we need to know about?" Emmie asked with a raised brow.

Gunner unzipped his jacket, revealing the cutest little piglet I'd ever seen. "My mom doesn't just breed Mastiffs. She breeds mini pigs too. This little girl is the runt of the litter. Ma's been bottle feeding her. I thought maybe... well, I thought she might cheer you up." He shrugged, looking mildly uncomfortable.

"Hell yes, she will," Emmie spoke for me, squealing with delight as Gunner handed her the piglet. "Oh my God, she's so cute," she crooned as she brought her over and placed her in my lap.

"I can take her back. I just thought...." Gunner trailed off.

"No." I smiled despite myself. "This is perfect. You're better at this than you think," I assured him.

I swore he blushed a bit at that.

"Yeah," Emmie agreed quietly. "You are."

The two of them shared a look that had Cash and me exchanging a raised brow in response before he waded in. "You guys got any beer? Ice cream ain't gonna cut it judging from the mood in this room."

"It's Ben and Jerry's, it'll cut it," Em assured him. "But yeah, we have beer."

A key sounded in the lock a moment before Grace walked in. "What's everyone doing?" she asked in confusion. "Is that a piglet? Or did I just have a really long day at work?"

I laughed. "Gunner and Cash are taking a shot at being therapists and brought a piglet and are now apparently opening beer," I informed her.

She sat down next to me, reaching for the pint as though bikers, ice cream, and a piglet were a perfectly normal combination. "Cherry Garcia, my favorite."

*   *   *

*Where are you?*

The text from Max came in close to midnight as I lay on the couch trying in vain to sleep. Cash and Gunner had left an hour ago, leaving the piglet I'd named Rosie with me. Emmie and Grace had gone to their rooms after I'd outright refused to take either of their beds.

It wasn't like I expected to get much sleep anyway.

I looked at his text, the mixture of relief that he was okay and anger at his tone a bewildering combination.

When my phone started to ring a moment later, I silenced it, anger winning out. He didn't get to talk to me the way he had and run off and then demand where I was.

"Seriously, Rosie, do yourself a favor and steer clear of cavemen, or... pigs," I whispered to the sleeping piglet in my lap. I'd fallen so in love with her, I wasn't sure what I'd do when it was time to give her back.

When he called again and again, I turned the damn thing off.

I flopped back down onto the couch, careful not to disrupt Rosie, and tried to fall asleep.

Emmie and Gracie both appeared in the hallway, looking

adorably sleepy. "Uh, Max has called me approximately one million times," Emmie shared dryly.

"I'm going on something close to that," Grace added.

"Shit. Sorry, guys," I muttered. "I didn't really want to talk to him tonight, but since he's calling you—" I was cut off by a hard rap at the front door.

Gracie raised a brow. "Guess you won't have to bother with your phone."

"I can talk to him if you want," Em volunteered.

"No, that's okay." I sighed, rising with Rosie in one hand. "I don't want to put you in the middle of this. Or more than you already are," I added.

"Good luck, girl." Gracie offered a thumbs-up before heading back to her room.

"He has his faults, but he loves you," Emmie murmured. She was rooting for her brother, and how could I blame her? "Night, Wren."

"Night, Em," I replied just as another knock, louder this time, sounded on the front door.

"Coming," I muttered.

I opened it, finding Max looking infuriatingly gorgeous on the other side. I expected him to explode at me for ignoring his calls. Instead, his gaze was full of remorse. "I'm sorry."

I stared at him in shock. I'd been prepared for a fight, but his heartfelt apology had me off balance.

He leaned on the doorframe, the muscles flexing in his arms. "I got a few hours out of town," he began solemnly. "At first, I couldn't think, couldn't feel," he admitted with an uncharacteristic openness I didn't dare suppress. "Then I could feel fucking *everything*. I shouldn't have left like that, shouldn't have said the things I did." He raked a hand over his overly long hair. "I've been fucked up over it all night. I swore I'd never hurt you, and I know I did, and..." His brow creased with near comical confusion as he looked at Rosie. "Is that a pig?"

"Yeah," I murmured. "Gunner brought her over."

His eyes returned to mine. "I'm sorry, Wren."

"I know you are. But it doesn't change anything, Max. Everyone accepts that you're a closed book, that you keep to yourself, that you don't share much. Your brothers, Emmie, even your parents. But not me. I can't." I shook my head. "If I can't have all of you, then I can't have any of you."

"You have all of me," he argued passionately.

I blinked back tears. "Do I?"

"What do I need to do here, Wren?"

I eyed him through tears, at a loss for words.

A look of determination crossed over his face. "You're my girl, Wren."

"I know it's not like you to open up. I know you don't want to talk about it, and if I thought you didn't need to, I'd let it lie. But today only proved that there's no way in hell you can go through what you did and keep it buried. If you don't want to talk to me, find someone you can talk to, because until you get all that out, until you do right by that little boy who had the weight of the world on his shoulders, then you won't be free to be mine. And, God, I want that, Max—no, I need it. More than anything."

His nostrils flared. "I am yours. And you damn well better know that you're mine."

Exhaustion, both mental and physical, had my shoulders sagging. "I need to get some sleep."

"Well, get the pig and let's go," he replied.

That statement would have been funny under different circumstances.

I wished it could be that simple. "I'm staying here tonight," I told him firmly. Nothing felt resolved, and yet there was nothing more to say.

His brow pinched, as though determining if he could hoist me and Rosie over his shoulder at the same time.

I put my hand on my waist, my eyes narrowed. "You'll give this to me, Max."

His head cocked to the side, assessing the level of challenge. "I'll give you anything, baby. Except a night away from me."

"Ugh, you are maddening." I groaned. "So, let me get this straight. You yell at me, take off on me, and then *I* don't get space?"

"Never promised to be perfect, baby." He stepped closer, and as always, angry or not, I was completely beguiled by him. "But I will swear to love you for the rest of my life." His word nearly dissolved the last of my resolve. "Now, I'm gonna take you home. You can be pissed at me. I earned that. But you'll do it next to me."

I looked at him a moment, gauging how likely I'd be to win if I continued to fight him. The set of his jaw and the determination in his gaze confirmed an inevitable loss.

"I'm taking the pig," I declared on a sigh.

His mouth quirked. "As long as you're comin', I don't give a shit if you bring a herd of goats home. Let's hit it."

Goats *were* pretty cute.

"One farm animal at a time, baby." He chuckled when he saw my face. "Let's go get what you need and head home."

I followed him inside, still angry, all while knowing that despite his faults, despite what we had to work out, being next to him was right where I was supposed to be.

# Chapter 29

## MAX

I knew she was awake. I could tell by her breath as she lay with her back to me, that damn pig nestled in her arms. The dogs had been curious last night when we'd come home, maybe even a bit jealous since Wren was clearly consumed with the little runt, but they'd quickly settled in and were now fast asleep on the floor. It was barely dawn, and I knew Wren had gotten about as much sleep as I had, which meant barely any at all.

I'd laid awake, consumed with the fact that the woman who was my whole fucking world doubted what she meant to me. I'd be damned if I didn't fix that, starting now.

"Come on, baby, want to take you some place," I coaxed quietly.

She looked at me warily over her shoulder. "Where?"

I shot her a warm smile. "Just get dressed. I'll go make us some coffee."

She grumbled a bit but rose to do as I asked as I made my way out to the kitchen.

When she emerged looking adorably sleepy, I handed her a traveler cup of coffee. "Ready?"

She nodded. "I crated Rosie. Hopefully she'll be okay. Will we be gone long?"

I shook my head, guiding her out to my truck.

Despite the lingering tension, we drove in comfortable silence. It was one of the countless things I loved about Wren. As a guy who didn't talk much, I'd always craved silence and solitude in my life. What I hadn't realized was that I just needed to find the right person to share it with.

When we pulled into the motel parking lot just off the freeway, she eyed me in obvious confusion.

I cleared my throat, wondering if this was all a bad idea. "You doubted you have all of me," I began by way of explanation. "I laid awake last night thinking of about a million different ways to prove to you that's bullshit. Short of taking you to New Mexico where I was born, this was the best I could come up with."

My eyes shifted toward the dilapidated building somehow still standing and in business after all these years. "This is where Janelle left Em and me those first few days in Hawthorne. I think she meant to take us to Jill but got strung out and forgot what she had planned." I stated this as fact, without emotion. "I haven't been here since," I admitted as her blue eyes lit with understanding. "It's not because I couldn't face it. I just didn't think I needed to," I explained quietly.

"I wanted to bring you here to make sure you know that there's nothing I'm keeping from you, no part of my mind that hasn't been touched by you, no part of my heart that isn't owned by you. That's not something I've ever experienced or will ever experience with anyone but you, so it's really fucking important that you get me."

Her eyes shone with tears as she nodded. "I get you, honey."

"For a long time, I honestly thought that part of my life was over and done with. I didn't spend any energy thinking about it. But falling in love with you has made me realize that maybe I should. Maybe there are parts of my childhood I haven't quite worked through. It's not that I'm holding anything back from you, more like I didn't know it was there in the first place. Does that make sense?"

Again, she nodded, the emotion clear on her face. She got me. Thank Christ.

"I'm hopin' you'll help me with that," I said, my voice low.

"I will," she murmured hoarsely.

"Now, yesterday, with the anger, I will check that," I swore, holding her eyes. "But honestly, that comes from a place of wanting to shield you. It's what I do—it's who I am. Obviously, I just don't always do it well. But you gotta know, that fury, it comes from a place that loves you so much I'd kill any motherfucker whoever did you wrong. I hated having her close to you. I don't want her to taint you. And God help her if she ever tried to get near our kids."

"You know you're not tainted, right?" she asked gently. "You know that no matter the decisions she made, they're no reflection on you or Emmie. That's her cross to bear. The fact she lost the opportunity to raise two amazing kids, it will haunt her, of that I have no doubt. But I don't want it to haunt you."

I reached my hand across the space between us, sweeping my thumb over that full bottom lip of hers I loved so much.

"I know. It won't."

"You're damn right," she replied passionately. "I won't let it."

Something warm settled in my gut, both pride for my fierce-as-hell woman but also comfort at knowing she'd always have my back. She'd fight for me just as I'd always fight for her.

"I know that, baby," I assured her. "Now let's get the fuck out of here," I grumbled, reversing the truck out of the lot and hoping that was the last time that shithole was ever in my line of sight. "Are we good?" I asked with a raised brow. I needed the words.

"Yeah." Her soft smile had me breathing a sigh of relief. "I hope Rosie's doing okay," she added, shifting topics.

"I'm sure she's fine. She is pretty cute."

"I already can't imagine giving her back." She sighed.

I had to smile at the fact that the woman I'd brought home not so long ago, who was unsure about my dogs and cat, now wanted to start her own farm. "I can talk to Gun about it if you want to keep her."

Her eyes popped wide in adorable wonder. "Really?"

I shrugged. "What the hell do we have all this land for if not to fill it? As long as you don't expect me to share a bed with a pig every night," I added. "Cute or not, the ham can sleep in her own bed. Starting tonight."

She rolled her eyes. "Fine."

*Got the address*

The text from Xander came through just as I was pulling up to the house, thinking of all the ways we could use said bed once we got inside. I inwardly groaned. This was the tip we'd been waiting on, and despite wanting nothing more than to keep Wren close to me, this wasn't something I could let another man handle. No, that asshole was all mine.

"Gotta make a quick call, baby," I told her reluctantly as I stayed seated in the truck.

She nodded, opening the door and hopping out. "See you inside."

I watched her head inside the house as I put the phone to my ear.

"Yo." I said by way of greeting when he picked up. 'Johnny get it for you?"

"Yep. This checks out, I just might let the little fucker live. We doin' this today?"

I gritted my teeth at the idea of leaving Wren. Every instinct protested it, but I ignored the urge, focusing instead on getting this over and done with. "Yeah. Get Mad and Cash. We'll ride out as soon as I get Wren secured."

"Got it. We'll wait for your word."

When I walked into the kitchen, Wren was cleaning up the dishes and chattering to the animals.

"Baby, gotta drop you at the club for a few hours."

She turned to me, her gorgeous blue eyes flashing with disappointment.

I sidled up to her, gently taking the plate from her and placing it in the sink so I could pull her close. "I hate fuckin' leaving you." I pressed my lips to her forehead. "But we might have a lead on where your stalker's living, and I have to check it out. I'll be back as soon as I can. In the meantime, I need to know you're safe."

She looked up at me and nodded in understanding. "But can I go to Liv's instead? I'm tired and just want to veg out.

Plus, I want to take Rosie. She'll think she's so cute." She smiled excitedly.

The thought of Axel having a piglet running around his house was fucking hilarious.

"All right, babe." I'd be more comfortable with her at the club, but I'd have given her just about anything she asked for just then.

Thirty minutes later, we were pulling up to Axel's. He would be at the bar for another hour, but Caleb, Maddox's younger brother, would keep an eye on the girls until he could get there. With the house having top-notch security, I felt about as good as I could about leaving her there.

"You okay, babe?" I asked her as we pulled up in front of the house. She'd been quiet on the way over, pensive.

She nodded, gazing out the window, appearing lost in thought.

I touched her cheek. "What is it?"

"I don't know what I'd do if anything ever happened to you." Her eyes were full of worry as she turned to look at me.

I cupped her delicate neck with my hand, offering a gentle squeeze. "Nothing will happen to me," I assured her. "I'm gonna put that asshole down, and we're gonna get on with our lives—together. Come here." I pulled her into my lap, threading my fingers in her hair to pull her mouth to mine. I didn't kiss her as long or hard as I dared, knowing I needed to let her go. "You want lasagna tonight?" I asked. It was her favorite.

She nodded readily.

I smiled at her enthusiasm. "Sounds like a plan. Be smart, all right?" I asked, trying not to show how much I dreaded leaving her. "Stay here until I come pick you up."

"I will."

"And if that pig shits in Axel's office, wouldn't be the worst thing," I added with a grin.

"Yeah right," she scoffed. "Like I'd let him make bacon out of Rosie."

I chuckled. He would too. "Love you, baby," I murmured, sweeping one last kiss over her lips.

"Love you too." She moved off my lap but paused before she slid out of the cab. "With fried pickles?" she asked with a lifted brow, referring to my lasagna.

I'd easily embraced the strange combinations of foods she liked. "Of course," I confirmed, as though affronted she'd even asked. I couldn't imagine what kind of weird shit I was going to have to come up with when I knocked her up. I looked forward to the challenge.

She smiled, sliding out of the cab and offering a sweet little wave. Damn but my girl got to me like nothing else.

I watched her go, hating how wrong it felt to let her walk away from me. It wasn't until she was safely inside the house, shutting the door with a quick wave, that I pulled down the drive, my gut clenching all the more with every mile I put between us.

"Fuck."

Beyond that, I was at a loss for words as I stood staring in fury at the walls of the unoccupied house we'd broken into. Wall after wall was covered in photos of Wren.

*My* Wren.

"Looks like he's been watching her for a long fucking time," Maddox grunted as he stepped closer to examine some of the photos. "Since high school at least." He looked at me, his expression calm—somebody fucking had to be. "You talked to her about past boyfriends and all that shit?"

"Yeah. She didn't really have any. That's what's made this so hard," I explained, trying like hell to rein myself in. The house was listed under a bogus corporation, a dead end. If I was going to be of any help at all, I had to calm down and try to think logically. "I'll call her, run through it with her again." Hopefully it would help, but honestly, I just needed to hear her voice after seeing this shit.

"You okay?" Her voice was full of worry when she answered on the first ring.

"Yeah, baby," I assured her, knowing I sounded tense as hell.

"It's bad?"

I couldn't lie to her. "It's not good. Pictures of you all over the place," I admitted as I heard the doorbell ring at Ax's. "This could be someone you know, baby. Can you try to think again of anyone who might have shown too much interest in you? Even something small might help."

"Jared Waters." Her tone was terrifyingly dull when she answered as though the life had been sucked right out of her. "He's here."

# Chapter 30

"Hang up," Jared commanded, a gun pressed to the back of Caleb's skull. I could hear Max hollering through the phone as I disconnected, setting it down on the counter.

"Fuck, Wren." Caleb's voice was full of remorse. "He and I played lacrosse together. I didn't think I—"

"Shut up," Jared ordered harshly as he turned to me, a chilling gleam lighting his gaze. "Let's go."

When I hesitated, he pointed the gun toward Liv. "You come with me or I put a bullet in her. She always wanted us to get together anyway." He grinned.

Olivia paled, looking at me helplessly.

"It's okay," I tried to assure her, even though we both knew it was far from it. "I'll come with you," I told Jared, the very idea making my stomach churn.

He waved the gun toward the front door, indicating that I should head that way. "Try anything and a bullet goes in her back," he warned Caleb, who looked ready to rip the man's heart out with his bare hands.

Now that I thought back on it, I remembered that he and Jared had been friendly in high school. It was no wonder he'd opened the door to him.

He pushed me toward a silver sedan, shoving me into the passenger seat. My heart hammered in my chest, my palms slick with sweat as I debated my next move. The minute I left this driveway with him, I knew my chances for survival plummeted. It was with that knowledge that I used the split second I had as he jogged to the driver's side to catapult out of the seat toward the woods.

My legs pumped as fast as I could go as the sound of gunfire boomed through the air. My leg exploded with pain as a bullet ripped through my calf. I stumbled as the boom of more gunfire erupted.

Jared appeared above me as I sat helplessly on the ground, unable to move. "You can come with me or die right here, your choice." He panted as I noticed a bloom of red appearing on his chest.

He'd been shot.

I stood up as he wrenched my arm toward him, pointing the gun on me as I limped after him. Caleb stood in the driveway, a gun aimed in our direction, his expression fierce.

He'd used my escape as an opportunity to fire on Jared, but now that I had a gun trained on me once again, his options were limited.

"Follow me and I'll kill her," Jared warned. After having no qualms about shooting me, I believed him.

This time, he shoved me through the driver's side, forcing me over the console as I cried out in pain. I streaked the upholstery with blood as I slumped into the passenger seat once again, clutching at my leg in agony.

As the engine fired up and Jared hit the gas, I watched Axel's house disappear in the sideview mirror, determined that this wouldn't be my last time seeing it. I'd survive this. I had to.

"Asshole shot me," Jared grunted, his hand clutching his chest as blood expanded across his chest and down his torso.

I looked down, watching as rivulets of blood slid down my leg, and didn't respond.

"We're not going far," he shared, and I didn't know if that was a good or bad thing. "I'll make sure to get you all bandaged up. You shouldn't have made me shoot you," he rebuked. "I only want to take care of you. I've waited so long for you to finally be mine."

I shivered at the yearning in his words as we hit the freeway.

"Where are we going?" I demanded through gritted teeth. I needed to get some sort of tourniquet on my leg right away, even if that meant arriving at whatever shop of horrors he had in store.

"Just a little place I've been fixing up for us," he answered. "We're nearly there."

He pulled off the freeway and onto a tree-lined street I'd driven through many times in my years in Hawthorne.

"Here we are," he announced proudly as he pulled into the driveway of a single-story home with a white picket fence.

I prayed someone, anyone, would see us as he held the gun trained on me, forcing me to walk ahead of him into the house.

The house was remarkable in how unremarkable it was. I'd expected something dark and dreary, for the walls to be covered in photos of me, something to indicate his obvious obsession. Instead, this looked like a perfectly ordinary home; it was charming even.

"I'll give you a tour later," he said as he pushed me gently toward a set of stairs off the kitchen. "I've got the master bedroom all decorated with your favorite colors, but for now, you'll need to stay down here until I can trust you not to run away again."

As we descended down the stairwell, dread swirled in my belly as we left the quaint kitchen and arrived in a basement outfitted with a floor-to-ceiling-sized cage.

"No!" I protested. "Don't make me go in there. I won't run away, I promise," I pleaded, eyeing the cell outfitted with a bed and toilet, feeling a fear I'd never known until that moment.

"It's just for a little while, sweetie," he crooned, opening the door and giving me a little shove inside.

The door shut with a resounding metal clang I felt all the way to my bones.

He sat on a nearby chair outside of the cell, and for the first time, I noticed how pale he was. "I just need to clean myself up." He sighed tiredly. "There are some fresh towels and a bucket of water for you to freshen up," he added, as though I was preparing for a night out rather than cleaning a bullet wound.

I didn't take the time to protest as I sat on the small bed and immediately dipped a towel into the nearby bucket. I needed to clean away some of the blood to get an idea of what I was dealing with. Not that that would tell me much. I wasn't a nurse.

The bucket quickly turned red with my blood as I dipped the towel repeatedly, finally able to see the quarter-sized wound. I could feel the bullet still lodged there. Was that good or bad? Should I try to pull it out? With what?

While I deliberated, I pulled a pillowcase off the nearby pillow, tying it just above my kneecap in hopes of staunching the blood flow.

When I looked at Jared again, his posture was slumped and his pallor had grown gray. "You're going to bleed to death," I informed him quietly. "You should call an ambulance."

He offered a shallow laugh in return. "You'd like that, wouldn't you? You were always looking for an excuse to get away from me. Even when I paid that idiot to rob you in that parking lot, you wouldn't even let me drive you home!" His gaze flared with anger before growing dull once more from blood loss. "Always too good for me. Well, not anymore. We're going to stay here together until you accept me. Until you love me the way that I love you."

Holy shit, he was so twisted.

"Rest up, sweetie." He sighed, shutting his eyes and leaning back in his seat. "I'm just going to take a little nap, and I'll be good as new."

Realization hit me with horrifying force. He was going to die and leave me trapped in this cage.

I stood up, grasping the bars with both hands. "Jared!" I cried, trying to rouse him. "You're dying. Let me out so I can help," I insisted.

He smiled serenely but didn't open his eyes. "I knew you'd want to take care of me the way that I want to take care of you, Wren."

"Jared!" I cried desperately, terror sweeping through me as the reality of my situation loomed.

He didn't respond, and after a moment, he started to slide toward the right, careening off the chair and collapsing on the ground in a heap.

He was dead. I knew it without doubt and yet, couldn't seem to believe it. For a few moments, I just stood there looking at his waxen form and tried to think clearly.

Desperation took over as I tried frantically to pull the iron bars apart. When that didn't work, I dumped the water out of the bucket and hurled it repeatedly at the bars, hoping for a weak spot, hoping to make a crack, a dent, anything.

Nothing worked.

I clung to the bars, my head drooped, chest heaving as the enormity of my situation loomed.

It was several moments before I could collect myself enough to take stock of my situation. The toilet had water, so at least I wouldn't die of thirst. I didn't have any food, and my leg was still oozing blood. How long could I survive down here? A few days? A week? How would anyone ever find me?

I sat on the edge of the bed and allowed myself to break down. The thought of dying down here, of never seeing Max again, of not having the life with him I'd wanted more than anything, was more than I could bare.

# Chapter 31

MAX

The ride back to Hawthorne was excruciating. Knowing Wren had been shot and was now dealing with a bullet wound and a psychopath had me on the brink of sanity myself. When we crested the road up to Axel's, the sun was dipping in the sky. His driveway was lined with bikes and familiar SUV's, the majority of the club having gathered no doubt to help how they could.

As I stalked into the house, my gaze immediately locked on Caleb and nothing else. Before I was even aware I'd moved, I had him by the throat and pressed to the nearest wall. "I trusted you to protect her!" I roared, my face inches from his. I wanted to tear him limb from limb for failing Wren, for failing me.

I distantly noticed through my rage-filled haze that he didn't fight me, but simply stood, seeming ready to accept whatever punishment I doled out.

A hand appeared on my shoulder, pressing firmly. "We don't have time for this," Sal's voice sounded in my ear.

"Leave him be and get your head on straight. Wren's waiting for you."

After a moment, I nodded, shoving Caleb away from me in disgust.

I turned to face the room full of my family and brothers. "What do we know?"

"Already went by the house he grew up in. It was sold a few years back, so that's a dead end," Gunner shared in frustration. It was in that moment, I realized that Wren wasn't just mine. No, my girl had worked her way into the hearts of the entire club throughout her life and more recently, when we'd gotten together. "Now that we know who we're dealing with, we've been learning what we can. X and Wes are out talkin' to some guys Caleb said he seemed tight with in school."

I shot another glare at Caleb before turning my attention back to Gun. "That's it?"

He shook his head, as though reluctant to share more. "I did some digging. He was locked up for a few years. I haven't had much time to get into the details, but it looks like he was stalking a woman at Penn State. He got locked up for failing to comply with a restraining order and a few other misdemeanors."

"That's why he didn't show up in Oregon until recently," I surmised. "Is that it?"

"For now." Gunner nodded reluctantly. "We're doing everything we can, man."

"Fuck." If there hadn't have been a couch behind me, I would have collapsed onto the ground as the sheer severity of the situation gripped me.

My mom sank to my side, wrapping an arm around me. "We're gonna find her, honey," she murmured. "And Wren's a fighter. She's not gonna give up, not when she knows you'll never give up on her."

"She's been shot," I rasped in torment. "We don't know how bad it is or where he took her. The thought of what she must be going through right now is making it hard to think past anything else."

"Well, you're going to have to," she replied steadily. "She needs you. And if anyone can figure this out, it's you." Her confidence in me was the motivation I needed.

I clenched my jaw, nodding once. My girl was out there somewhere waiting on me to find her, and I'd be damned if I let her down.

\* \* \*

At dawn, I stood out on my back patio, staring blankly out at the tree line. It had been a sleepless night that had brought no new information. There was no way I could sleep, not while Wren was out there somewhere.

When the slider opened behind me, I didn't turn, but instead watched in my periphery as Sal leaned against the railing alongside me.

"Figured you'd be up. Your mom let me in," he explained, his tone as gruff as always but with a raw edge that was new.

I nodded. My mom and Emmie had spent the night. I couldn't get rid of them if I'd tried, and I hadn't.

For a while, we just stood side by side, watching the sun rise further in the sky, lighting the tree line with a rose-colored hue. "She was determined from the moment she was born. Our stubborn little raven-haired girl with eyes as big as saucers. Shit, she was gorgeous," he murmured, his tone taking on a reverence that painted a picture I could almost see. "Wanted to do everything herself." He chuckled. "Kat and I tried for years to have another one, but we couldn't make it happen, and after a while, we realized that Wren was more than enough. She was always enough," he said, and I wondered if he was speaking to himself or to me.

"She was defiant, but not in the way most kids are. She just wanted to do things her own way, and if that meant doing things that boys typically did, then so be it. I'll never forget her marching out to our garage, she must have been six or seven, wearing her little pink dress she loved so much with a tool box in her hand." He chuckled at the memory. "She demanded I show her how to fix up a car. So, I did." He shrugged. "And shit if she wasn't better than me before she was a teenager."

"Doesn't surprise me." I shook my head, thinking of all the times Wren had proven how goddamn special she was. I swallowed hard against the emotion clawing at my insides. "Should have put a ring on her finger," I lamented, dropping my head and leaning back on my arms. "I was waiting. Why did I wait?"

"You'll have plenty of time for that," he assured me. "We have years ahead of us to fight over who gets the first dance at your wedding, and you'll get pissed when Kat and I steal your babies once you have them. I've already planned on years of you being a pain in my ass, can't have that preparation goin' to waste."

I looked up at him in surprise as he offered a pained smile.

"I definitely get the first dance," I shot back, a ghost of a smile tugging at my lips.

He eyed me intently for a moment before he nodded. "Yeah, Max, you do."

"I'll take care of her." It was important to me that he knew that—that he believed it.

"I know you will." He nodded, clapping me on the back. "She chose well." The note of pride in his tone had me swallowing hard against emotion.

I simply nodded, unable to reply as he lifted his chin toward the house. "I think your mom put some coffee on."

It was a good thing too, because I'd need a pot or two of it. Today, I was bringing my girl home.

My living room was full of Knights members by the time I was on my second cup. Most of them had been up all night as well, trying to do anything they could to figure out where Wren had been taken or might be headed.

Gunner, Cash, and I were trying to find more links to Jared when Maddox strode in, an unfamiliar brunette in tow.

I looked at him in confusion since this wasn't the time to be bringing strangers around, and I expected him to know it.

The girl looked nervous, hanging close to Maddox as he kept a protective hand on her lower back.

"What's goin' on?" I asked.

"This is Francesca," he introduced. "She might know where Jared would take Wren."

My gaze sharpened on her as hope and distrust waged a war inside me. "You're the source."

She bit her lip, looking up at Maddox for guidance. At his nod, she spoke, her voice soft. "I am."

"And how would you know where Jared would take Wren?" I demanded. She'd mislead us before; I wasn't about to let that happen again.

She took a deep breath. "Jared uses his mother's maiden name. His father is Angelo Rossi."

I took a step back, floored by what she'd just shared. "And you know this because...?"

"Because Rossi is my last name too," she murmured.

The room erupted with questions and tension after she'd dropped her little bomb. Maddox pulled her protectively into his body, his expression deadly. "Everyone chill the fuck out," he barked. "Frannie's on our side. She's risking her life being here, going against her family so she can help Wren. Shut the fuck up and listen."

He was right. All I cared about was finding Wren.

Francesca licked her lips nervously, and it was clear she wanted to be anywhere but here. Whatever her motives were, whether they were pure or not, I'd take any information she had.

"Jared and I aren't close. I had no idea he was stalking your girlfriend until Maddox came to me on the off chance I might know something. When he showed me a picture of Jared, I couldn't believe it," she admitted shakily. "I don't know where he took her or what he has planned, but I overheard him bragging a few months back about a house he bought in Hawthorne that he was fixing up for his girl."

I glowered at her words but forced myself to remain silent.

"I don't have the address, but he said it was in the Windsor Park neighborhood."

"Could be something," Gunner spoke up, already in investigative mode. Out of all of us, he was always best with that shit. "I can look up the real estate records and narrow down which places were sold in that time frame."

I nodded, urgently hoping like hell this was the lead we needed.

Cash cocked his head to the side, visibly sizing up Francesca. "You told Mad the Rossis were planning a drop, when really Jared had an attempted kidnapping planned. How do you explain that?"

Maddox growled, clearly ready to take on anyone who questioned her. "It's okay, Maddox," she assured him softly before turning her eyes to Cash. "I think my family suspects something and purposefully fed me that information. It's why I'm here. I think my cover is blown regardless."

If that was true, then she was in a hell of a lot of danger. Maddox's posture and expression proved he already knew this.

"Why risk it?" Cole asked, speaking for the first time. His tone wasn't skeptical but curious, as I was sure we all were.

"I have my reasons." She shrugged, her gaze sliding to the side.

Gunner set his laptop aside, his gaze locking with mine. "I think I might have something."

I was grabbing my keys before he'd even finished the sentence. I looked to Sal; if he wanted to ride out with us, I'd never deny him that.

He wrapped an arm around Kat, his eyes on me. "Go get our girl."

# Chapter 32

## WREN

It had been a hellish night. When night fell, the small amount of light that had been coming in through the small basement window disappeared, leaving me to suffer the night in pitch black. Sleeping in a cell with a dead body slumped next to it, my stomach growling and calf burning, was a waking nightmare. My mind had gone to some outlandish places as the night stretched.

At one point, I'd sworn I heard music, and in another, Jared breathing—that had been the scariest of all. But as day break allowed a small sliver of sun to light my surroundings, Jared was still slumped in the same position, his face a ghoulish gray.

I shivered at the very sight of him.

Lying back down on my small bed and curling into the fetal position, I conjured an image of Max in my mind as I had tried to do throughout the night. I pictured that slow smile of his that I loved so much, those warm brown eyes. I imagined his arms around me now, pulling me close, kissing my temple as he liked to do.

A noise overhead woke me from a light sleep. At first, I dismissed it as my mind playing tricks on me. Then I heard it again, louder this time.

I sprang out of bed, wincing at the pain in my leg. "Hello?" I shouted, my voice hoarse from lack of sleep and thirst. I hadn't gotten desperate enough to drink out of the toilet yet. "I'm down here!" I hollered as loud as I could.

I tried yelling throughout the night, hoping a neighbor would hear me, to no avail. I was scared to hope this would be different.

The heavy tread of feet on the stairs sounded a moment before Max came into view. I'd never seen a more beautiful sight.

Relieved tears filled my eyes as I clung to the bars, trying to hold myself up.

His gaze swung from me to Jared's corpse before returning to me. "Baby." His tone was guttural. "Gonna get you out of there," he swore as Gunner and Cash appeared in the room.

"Do you know where the key is?" he asked me, and despite the urgency in his gaze, his tone was calm. I knew the effort it must have taken him.

"He has them." I pointed to Jared with a grimace.

Cash didn't hesitate, and as Max stood in front of me, holding my hands through the bars, he dug through a dead man's jeans. "Found 'em," he replied a moment later, dangling them from his fingers.

"Damn, remind me not to kidnap you, Wren. Everyone who tries ends up dead." Gunner shot me a wry grin. He was trying to put me at ease, and to the degree that it was possible, it worked.

Max's growl of discontent proved he didn't appreciate the gesture.

After they tried a few keys, finally the sound of the lock snicking open sounded, and a heartbeat later, Max had me in his arms.

He lifted me bridal style. "Close your eyes. I don't want you looking at this fuckin' place a second longer," he grunted as he headed for the stairs.

I didn't argue, eager to erase the dungeon from my mind—though I didn't think that would actually ever be possible.

I only opened them when we were outside, the fresh air of the morning calming my frazzled nerves. Max placed me in the passenger seat of his truck, leaning toward me, his forehead pressed to mine. "Jesus fuck, fuck," he chanted. When I pressed my hands to his shoulders, they were coiled tight. He took a few deep breaths before he stepped back a pace to peer down at me. "Do you have any other injuries?"

He wanted to know if Jared touched me.

I shook my head. "He died yesterday, almost immediately after he locked me in that cell." I shivered, knowing how much worse it could have been.

Some of the tightness in his body eased at that news.

"We have to get that leg seen to. I'd be more comfortable taking you to Tag's. Laurie can take care of you there. I just... I need to keep you close. I need to know I can get to you." His voice was pained as he struggled to explain himself.

I placed my hand on the side of his neck, relishing the feel of his pulse thumping under my skin. "That's fine."

I looked over Max's shoulder at the quaint little house that had been my own personal house of horrors. "What are you going to do about him?" I asked quietly.

"Don't worry about it," Max was quick to assure me. "All you need to focus on is that he's gone. It's over. Finally." He exhaled.

"Finally," I agreed as a look passed over his face that I couldn't place. It almost looked like regret.

"Just wish I could've put that asshole down myself," he explained. "Was lookin' forward to that. Let's get you out of here." He gently guided me further into the truck, closing the door for me.

"I don't get it," I murmured in confusion as we pulled away from the curb. "He barely even talked to me. He asked me out a few times in high school, but it's not like he even really tried to date me." I shook my head in bafflement. "Aside from hiring that guy to attack me in the parking lot and wanting to look like a savior or something, he kept his distance."

Max's forearm tensed on the wheel as he glanced over at me briefly. "He was fucking twisted, babe. Who knows how his mind worked? Probably better to try not to think about it."

That was easier said than done, and we both knew it.

"Are my parents okay?" I asked.

He nodded. "Your pop was way calmer than me," he admitted. "The entire club rallied. No one slept, barely ate. We weren't going to quit until we found you." He glanced at me again, his eyes flashing. "I would have never quit, Wren."

"I know." And I did. I'd never doubted it. "How did you find me?"

"Mad has a source," he replied simply, and I sensed he

didn't want to get into it now. That was fine by me. Now that I was safe, exhaustion was setting in with full force.

When we pulled up in front of Tag and Laurie's two-story home, I was somewhere between sleep and wakefulness. Max had me in his arms before I was even aware he'd stopped the truck.

I opened my eyes, blearily noting Laurie's petite form peeking out from behind her massive husband.

"Oh dear," she greeted with concern when she got a look at me. "Let's get you inside."

"Holy shit, that's a lot of blood!" a young voice cried from the couch when we entered the living room. Seated beside his sisters, Talon was staring at us with an open mouth.

"Mouth, Talon," Laurie chastised.

"Sorry, Ma," he muttered, turning his eyes back to the TV as the girls giggled.

"Don't let your brother give you any ideas." Tag looked pointedly at the girls as he followed us into the kitchen where Laurie sat me in a chair.

"Three must be a bit of a handful," I commented, needing to fill the tense atmosphere with conversation. Laurie snorted as she dug around in a first aid kit. "We had twins, and then this one just had to have one more." She shot a playful look at her husband.

"Takes two, baby," Tag grinned. "As I remember, I didn't have to work too hard to convince you."

Laurie blushed adorably, and I marveled that they were still so in love with each other.

"Three doesn't sound so bad." Max shrugged as he leaned against the counter, watching Laurie prep her supplies.

My head snapped to his in surprise. We'd never talked about children. "Oh yeah? You gonna carry them?" I asked dryly.

His lips tipped up, eyes flashing with humor.

Laurie appraised me with a raised brow. "Men," she muttered with a wink. "All right," she continued as I laughed and Tag mock growled. "Let's get this cleaned up and see what we're working with." She gently washed away the rest of the dried blood. "You did a great job with this, Wren," she commended as she removed the tourniquet still tied around my thigh. I'd been afraid to remove it. "I'm going to need to remove this bullet. I'll give you something to numb the area."

Max moved to my side, taking my hand as she produced a needle that was way too big for my liking.

"Eyes on me, baby," Max commanded gently, and I lifted my eyes to his.

I winced as an incredible sting hit my calf.

"I'm sorry, sweetheart," Laurie murmured.

"How's Rosie?" I asked Max through gritted teeth.

Max looked down at me, stroking my hair back, and from the look in his eyes, I knew she'd gotten to him too. "Fine. She wasn't hurting for love, believe me. Frank's a bit jealous."

"He shit in the tub again?"

"Yep."

I laughed despite myself. "Figures."

"You still want lasagna tonight?" he asked softly.

"That sounds amazing. I'm actually starving," I admitted, my hunger returning full force at the mere thought.

"Start with this," Laurie suggested, placing a banana in my hand. Max reached out to grab it, peeling it for me.

I didn't think anything had ever tasted so good once he handed it to me. I forced myself not to eat it in two bites.

"You're probably dehydrated. Tag, get her some water, would you?" she asked her husband.

A second later, a glass of water was placed in my hand, which I promptly tipped back, chugging the contents. I hadn't realized how thirsty I was. He took it back to refill it.

"Just about done," she informed me, and I looked down at her in surprise.

I'd always known Laurie was good. Along with Jill and Scarlet who were also nurses, she'd been stitching up members of the club for years and had been head nurse at the hospital for over a decade. But that had still been crazy fast.

"Your body already did most of the hard work," she explained with a warm smile. "Just needed to clean you up and get that bullet out. You'll be sore for a while, but you should heal without any complications. Anything comes up, you know where to find me." She placed a bandage over the wound.

"Max, a word," Tag requested, cocking his head toward the other room.

When Max seemed reluctant to leave me, I squeezed his hand. "I'm fine, babe. We're about done here anyway."

He blew out a breath, nodding once. "I'll be right back," he replied as he followed Tag out of sight.

"Phew. I remember those days." Laurie smiled after him.

"What days?"

"The beginning." She sighed blissfully. "Tag all but carried me over his shoulder with a club in his hand when we started dating." She laughed. "Sometimes he still does," she confided with a whisper.

I laughed, hoping when we were their age that we still had the same passion they clearly did.

It was only a moment later that Max returned. "She'll be fine," Laurie informed him at the look of worry on his face. "Just keep weight off her leg for a little while and make sure she gets plenty of liquids."

Max nodded. "Thanks, Laurie."

"Any time."

"I'll catch up with you later," Max told Tag as he swept me up into his arms, preparing to walk us out. I had a feeling he'd be wanting to carry me for the near future. I didn't plan to argue.

Tag nodded before his eyes turned to me. "Glad you're all right, honey."

"Thanks, Tag."

Max gently deposited me back in the passenger side of the truck, kissing my forehead. "Let's get you home."

I sighed blissfully. Nothing had ever sounded better.

# Chapter 33

He kept my hand in his for the entire drive home, and I had no doubt he'd have pulled me into his lap if that was safe. I stared out the window, feeling exhausted, hungry, and otherwise numb. The past twenty-four hours felt so surreal, like someone else's nightmare.

"Everyone is still here?" I yelped in alarm when we'd pulled up the driveway, which was packed with bikes and SUVs.

Max looked over at me, concern clear in his eyes. "They're just worried about you, baby."

"I know," I murmured. "I'm just... I'm not ready. I feel like I can't...." I struggled to find the words to convey the torrent of emotions swelling up inside me.

He cupped my neck gently. "Okay, babe. I've got you, don't worry," he soothed. "I'm gonna carry you inside and tell everyone you're not up to visitors right now. Okay?"

"Okay," I breathed in relief. Facing their worry all at once was more than I could handle at the moment.

He came around the side of the truck, sweeping me up in his arms. I clung to his shoulders, burying my face in his neck, breathing in his delicious and soothing scent.

Our living room erupted with noise the moment we stepped inside.

Max held a hand up to halt the clamor. "Appreciate the concern. Wren's okay but not feeling great. I'm going to get her to bed, and she'll see you all soon," he announced without preamble. Without waiting for a reply, he strode back toward the master bedroom.

Part of me felt guilty for not trying to assuage what had to be a very worried room of friends and family, but in that moment, I just needed to shroud myself in a cocoon and pull Max into it.

He walked into the bathroom, setting me on the counter, resting his hands on either side of me. "Figured you'd want a shower," he murmured, peering into my eyes. At my nod, he turned on the water before removing his tee shirt.

I tracked his movements, watching avidly as his skin revealed itself to me. Once he'd removed all his clothes, he started on me, gently pulling my tee shirt up over my head, standing me up to slide my shorts down my legs, careful to avoid my bandage. Every movement was deliberate and deliciously slow.

I basked in the warmth of his hands on me.

He guided us into the shower, his back to the spray as wrapped his arms around me. "Your leg okay like this?"

I nodded against his chest, not wanting anything to disrupt this moment. When the first sob escaped, it racked my entire frame with its intensity. Max only held me tighter, kissing the top of my head. Once I started, I couldn't seem to stop. I'd thought I was going to die in that cell, looking at a dead psychopath.

Max didn't try to talk to me. He didn't try to tell me it was okay. Instead, he did the only thing I really needed; he held me close until my sobs turned to hiccups and I was too exhausted to produce any more tears.

Only then did he tilt my head back to look at him. I was sure I looked frightful with makeup running down my face and puffy eyes, but the look of adoration on his face pushed that worry from my mind.

"You're here with me, baby. We get to live our forever together. It's over. It's over," he repeated, and I knew he was reminding himself just as much as me.

I nodded fervently, wanting to cling to thoughts of the future rather than the nightmare of the past.

"When your mind wants to take you to a dark place, you think about that," he told me. "You think about the life we get to have together."

"Okay, Max," I agreed readily.

He kissed me then, slow and sweet, as though rediscovering my mouth. His teeth nipped at my lower lip, his hands grasping my backside as I moaned into his mouth.

"I need you," I whispered desperately.

His shoulders tensed under my fingertips. "Baby, your leg...." His protest was muffled, his lips against my skin.

"Fuck my leg," I argued passionately, and he pulled back, looking down at me in surprise.

"I just spent the past twenty-four hours thinking I might not get another chance to be with you," I explained through a fresh sheen of tears. "I imagined you holding me. I pictured your hands." My fingers moved to entwine with his, "I heard your voice. You helped get me through, and you weren't even there. But now, you're actually here, under my hands, and... I need you to take it all away. I need you," I repeated. "Please."

"If only you hadn't said please," he growled.

My knees turned weak at the predatory gleam in his eye.

He lifted me effortlessly, my legs wrapping around his trim waist as he pressed me against the shower wall.

"Marry me," he rasped, his face buried in my neck.

"What?" I honestly wasn't sure I'd heard him right.

He pulled back to look me in the eye. "Marry me, Wren."

"You're serious?" I marveled. Everything felt so surreal.

"I've never been more serious about anything in my life," he said with that trademark intensity I loved about him so damn much.

"You're my everything, baby. And I've given you all of me and want to keep doing it until the day I die. Nothing has ever felt better. You light up my whole goddamn world. You accept me as I am, but you push me at the same time. I need you. But more importantly, I want you. Marry me."

"Yes!" I cried emphatically, my voice ricocheting off the tile.

His answering grin stopped my heart before sending it into overdrive. "Yeah?"

I nodded, grinning from ear to ear. "Yeah."

He kissed me then with a ravenous hunger I never wanted to fully satiate. "You're gonna be my wife," he growled as he thrust inside me, my answering moan echoing off the shower walls. "I'm going to love you until the day I die. I'm going to live my life to make you so fucking happy." His body took mine with a sense of ownership, of worship that had my head spinning.

I grasped his head between my hands, forcing him to look at him. I had nothing to say; I just needed to see his face, to see his eyes as he claimed me.

The shower wall was cold and unforgiving against my back, the man inside me hard as steel, and yet, I'd never felt so warm or languid in my life.

"You finish school, gonna put a baby in you," he grunted.

I nodded, unable to form words.

"Fuck, baby, get there," he gritted out, the muscles in his arms and shoulders deliciously tense as he took me.

I wrapped my legs around him tighter, pulling him closer, as he brought me to that teasing edge, the one I loved to hate. I wanted to balance just a bit longer, and yet I couldn't wait to fall over it. Moments later, I tumbled into free fall, calling his name as I went.

His control slipped as his movements grew frantic seconds before he growled my name, holding himself deep inside me with a roar of contentment.

"Fuck," he clipped, his breathing ragged as he bit my neck gently. "Are you okay?" His gaze was worried as he pulled back to look at me.

"I'm so beyond okay," I practically slurred.

"I'm gonna get you to be bed." He stepped out of the shower with my legs still wrapped around his waist. I rested my head on his shoulder, content to let him take care of me.

The click of nails on the hardwood and a tiny snort had me lifting my head.

"I think the ham missed you." Max chuckled.

I smacked his arm. "Stop calling her that. And we're not eating bacon ever again."

He raised a brow. "Maybe you're not."

I huffed as he threw a towel down and set me gently on the edge of the bed gently drying me off. "Gonna get that wound redressed," he mumbled, stalking off toward the bathroom. I watched him go, practically salivating over his delicious backside despite the fact that I'd just had him.

That hunger went both ways.

"Hi, Rosie," I murmured, bending to pick up my sweet little hambone. She wriggled and snorted in my arms as I kissed her.

The dogs and cat looked on with mild annoyance until I made sure to give them some love.

"They missed you," Max murmured with a sad smile. I hadn't even realized he was watching from the doorway as I made goofy faces at the dogs. He dropped to my feet, carefully removing my wet bandage and replacing it with a dry one before coaxing me to sit back as he put the covers over me. "Eat this," he coaxed handing me a sandwich. "Then you need to get some rest."

I yawned huge. "I do," I agreed. "But you'll lie down with me, right?" I asked in mild alarm. I needed him close.

His brows lifted. "If you think you're getting more than a wall away from me in the near future, we're gonna have to get straight here, babe. And trust me, it's more for my sanity than yours."

Well, I guess that answered that.

He put Rosie in her crate as I polished off my sandwich, gesturing for the dogs to their beds before he crawled in beside me, pulling me close. "Sleep, baby."

I nodded, snuggling deeper into him. Despite the sun peeking through the blinds, I knew I could.

The past twenty-four hours still clung to my skin, still tingled at the back of my mind like an itch, but I knew that, with it finally over, I'd have the future I'd always wanted. It was with that simple sense of joy, of a life spent with a gloriously complex man, that I was able to fall asleep.

# *Chapter 34*

## MAX

I was fighting like hell not to pace a hole in the floor two weeks later as I waited for Sal.

"Did you have too much coffee again?" Wren accused, noting my energy.

"Must've," I lied, forcing myself to appear casual. "Wasn't Liv supposed to be here soon?" I prompted. I needed her out of here in order to pull this off.

After spending the past few weeks only leaving her side for one reason, I was finally ready to share the surprise Sal and I had been working on.

"Yeah," she replied, looking at me skeptically as she left the room with Frank, Rosie, and both dogs in tow, a now constant sight.

Gunner's mom had readily agreed to us keeping Rosie. Now, I just needed to get Wren off her wanting a whole farm kick. I'd caught her looking at miniature horses online the night before.

The fact we had a goddamn pig was enough. Though I had to admit, she was cute as hell.

"Liv just texted. She's pulling up," she announced as she reappeared, her hair still wet from an earlier shower, looking fucking beautiful in blue jeans and a white tank top. I loved the rare occasions where she dressed up, but I thought she was most beautiful as she was now, dressed casually with little to no makeup marring her gorgeous skin. "Hopefully I can actually pass this test." She wrinkled her brow.

She'd been able to register late for fall semester. She was playing catch up, but my girl was determined.

"You'll do great," I assured her, dipping to kiss her lips and tweaking the engagement ring I'd placed there weeks before. "We went over all your notes last night. You knew them backwards and forwards, don't sweat it."

"Okay," she replied breathlessly, swaying into my kiss. "Maybe I'll just stay here and we can go to bed."

I chuckled. "Tempting, but you'd be pissed at me later if I took you up on that." I swatted her ass as she pouted over her shoulder, headed out the door to meet Liv.

Even now, weeks later, it was hard for me to watch her go, to let her be away from me. But I knew I needed to. The business with Jared was over and done with. She needed to reclaim her life in Hawthorne, and some of that had to be without me.

"I'll see you tonight." She smiled coyly over her shoulder at me.

*Sooner than that, baby.* I thought, as I fought a grin.

It was only a short time after I'd heard Liv's car pull out of our drive that the rumble of a motor sounded. I bolted for the door, finding Sal cutting the engine on Wren's Mustang that, unbeknownst to her, we'd finished the upgrades on.

The car looked fucking sweet. We'd kept it as original as possible while finishing up the plans she and Sal had come up with together. As far as she knew, I was still against her driving it. Though I'd still love to see her behind the wheel of something even safer, vintage cars were a passion of Wren's, and I knew I'd have to meet her in the middle.

I caught the keys midair after he threw them.

"We doin' dinner tonight?" he asked with a lifted brow as Kat pulled up the drive to pick him up. It had become a bit of a tradition that we grilled at Sal's place on Thursday nights.

"Yep," I agreed.

Kat leaned out the window with a grin. "She's gonna be so excited."

I nodded. "We'll be by later," I said in parting, watching as Sal strode toward Kat's car.

After a brief argument, where he obviously insisted on driving, she moved to the passenger seat, huffing about alpha men the entire time.

I grinned at their antics, watching as they pulled away before I made my way back into the house to grab my jacket.

I grinned as I fired up the Mustang, it's throaty throttle like music to my ears. The sun was shining with just a hint of the chill of winter starting to creep into the late afternoon as I pulled onto the highway, cranking the stereo. It was a few hours before Wren was done with school, but I was too fired up to sit around and wait.

The club was just as good a place as any to kill time.

"Nice ride," Mad commented, headed for his bike when I pulled into headquarters a few minutes later.

"It's Wren's," I replied as I cut the engine and climbed out. "You outta here?"

"Yeah."

It wasn't lost on me that Mad had seemed troubled the last few weeks. He'd always been on the serious side, but this was something different. I leaned against the side of the car, my arms crossed. "You good?"

His eyes slid to the side.

"You worried about your girl?" I guessed. It was no secret he'd claimed the Rossi girl. Whether or not she claimed him back was something else entirely.

"How could I not be fuckin' worried?" he shot back. "She risked her life to save Wren's. Those assholes know she worked with us. And it's not like she's getting the warmest reception from our side either," he scoffed. "She thinks everyone hates her. She's keepin' her distance right when I need to keep an eye on her." He looked at me, his gray eyes blazing. "If those assholes lay a hand on her, they'll answer to me."

"We have your back on that, brother," I assured him firmly. There might be some lingering lack of trust when it came to Francesca and the family she came from, but if she mattered to Mad, then she mattered to all of us.

"Appreciate it." He nodded, throwing a leg over his bike. "Gonna go see if I can get my stubborn woman to stay with me."

I bit back a smile, knowing something about stubborn females myself. "Good luck."

He snorted, firing up his bike. With a final two-fingered salute, he roared off down the road.

The club was quiet when I walked in, the only sound the pool balls clacking together as Gunner and a prospect played in the corner. After a nod in their direction, I headed down the hall, finding Cole in his office scowling at something on his phone.

"What's good?" I asked, plopping down in the seat across from him.

He heaved a breath, shoving his phone away from him. "Same shit, different day."

I cocked my head to the side. "Something I can help with?"

"The Rossi's don't fall in line, then yes. For now, no." He shook his head as he sat back in his chair regarding me. "You seem good," he assessed, his bright blue eyes zeroed in on me with his typical intensity.

"I am."

"You were always quiet," he mused. "But sometimes I wondered if it was because you were holdin' back, holding something in. I don't get that from you anymore."

"Still working on it," I admitted. "Wren's helping. She pushes me when I need it."

He nodded. "A good woman will accept who you are. But the best will push you to be even better."

I couldn't have agreed more.

"You get word that Janelle left town?"

The question caught me momentarily off guard. I hadn't been keeping tabs on her, but I wasn't surprised Cole had been. "I didn't." I shook my head. "Not surprised."

He nodded, his fingers steepled against his chin as he regarded me. "You didn't go and see her." It wasn't a question.

My instinct was to say no and let it lie, to avoid the conversation all together, but then I remembered what I'd told Wren, that I'd promised to try.

"I didn't see the point." I shrugged. "Nothing to work out with her, and I have no interest in hearing what she has to say."

"You didn't have anything to say to her? She's lucky I didn't go have a few words with her myself." He glowered.

"She doesn't deserve the time it would take me, and plus, any closure I might need wouldn't be solved in talking to her. I think it's more talking it out with Wren—and with you."

He nodded thoughtfully. "Anytime, you know that."

"I do," I agreed, rising to stand. "Gotta go pick up Wren."

"She's gonna be fucking thrilled." He grinned. Most of the guys were in on the surprise since Sal and I had worked on it at the club for the past few weeks.

"Hope so," I replied, tapping his desk once. "I'll catch you later."

"Later."

"Cole." I paused in the doorway, waiting for his eyes. "Thanks."

He smiled, his eyes warm. "You're welcome."

I pulled into the community college a few minutes early, wanting to make sure I beat her to the parking lot. She thought Olivia would be driving her home.

I leaned against the car, searching the students milling around, eager to lay eyes on my girl. It had only been a few hours and still felt like it had been way too long.

Then I saw her, walking toward me, laughing at something Liv was saying as Tatum chuckled along with them. She was so fucking gorgeous, she stole my breath on a daily basis. The minute she caught sight of me, her blue eyes lit with excitement that made me feel ten feet tall.

Then she saw the car and I heard her shriek from across the lot.

I grinned at her exuberance as she ran toward me. "How did you...? When did you...?" she sputtered as I took her in my arms. "You've barely left my side."

I kissed her temple. "Some of those club meetings weren't for real. Your dad and I worked on it together."

Her eyes popped wide in surprise. "I thought you didn't want me to drive it?" she demanded excitedly as she opened the driver's side door and climbed inside. I sat beside her in the passenger side, smiling with pride as she admired the interior.

"We'll just leave you to it." Liv winked, linking arms with Tatum as they strode toward her car.

I shot her a grateful nod. Liv was always looking out for my girl, and for that, I'd always have her back.

"I'd still rather have you in something safer," I admitted, turning my attention back to Wren. "But I know you love this car. As long as you promise me you'll drive safely, then if it makes you happy, you know I'd do anything to make that happen."

She looked at me with tears shining in her eyes. "I do know that."

"All right, now switch with me, baby," I told her.

"This is my car, and I just got it back. I'm driving." She shook her head.

Damn, she was cute when she thought she was about to win an argument.

"Baby, I'm in a car, I'm driving, you know this," I answered patiently. "But you also know I'd make an exception this time if your leg wasn't still sore," I added, looking pointedly at her calf.

"Ugh, if that weren't true, I wouldn't back down so easily." She huffed, climbing out of the car. When she arrived at the passenger's side, I pulled her gently into my lap, loving her little shriek of delight.

"I'll make it worth your while," I promised, sliding my nose along her neck, my cock hardening at her delicious scent and the little whimper that escaped her lips. I shifted, putting her ass in the seat and standing up before I took her right there in the parking lot.

The deep rumble of the engine had Wren bouncing in delight as I put the car in gear. I glanced over at her with a grin before hitting the gas.

"Gotta swing by the store. Then we're headed to your folk's house," I informed her.

"And we're going to the store because you think Pop didn't buy the right steak?" she guessed correctly.

Sal was good at a lot of things, but he couldn't grill for shit. My lip twitched. "Right."

Her hand made its way to my thigh, resting comfortably as I drove us through town.

"Have you talked to Caleb?" she asked gently.

She'd been pushing the topic ever since Caleb had let that fucker into his house. Somehow, my girl had forgiven him right away. I wasn't nearly there. I wasn't sure I'd ever be.

"No," I ground out.

"Honey—"

I shook my head, cutting her off. "He could have gotten you killed because he didn't use his fucking head. I'm not ready to forgive that shit. I don't know if I ever will be."

She squeezed my thigh, and I knew she'd let the subject drop, for now. My girl knew me well. She knew when to push and when to let me work things through on my own time.

I turned to glance her way as we idled at a red light. "Your mom's pretty intense about this wedding shit," I noted dryly.

She groaned. "Don't remind me. You'd think I was the queen of England or something. Maybe we should just elope."

"Tempting." I chuckled as I hit the gas when the light turned green. "But we can't do that, and you know it. This is important to your mom, and to your pop. He's just not as vocal about it. There's only one time to plan their only daughter's wedding."

"Yeah, I know," she grumbled. "But if I have to look at one more bridal magazine, I'm going to lose it.

"I'll talk to Sal, get him to talk to her," I assured her.

Sal and I had developed an even closer bond than we'd had before I claimed Wren. Through my relationship with Wren, I'd gained not only the love of my life but another family I loved nearly as much as my own.

"He listens to you." She leaned back on the headrest, looking peaceful.

It was a new chapter for us, being able to relax. The shit with the Rossis was by no means dealt with, but my girl was safe. We were finally free to just... be.

"I'll buy some pineapple since you like it with your steak," I said, trying not to grimace.

"It's good!" she protested, swatting my arm, no doubt having caught my expression.

"Whatever you say, baby." I chuckled. "Can't wait to see what kind of wedding cake you come up with."

She rolled her eyes, but the pink tinge to her cheeks told me she already had some weird-ass ideas.

The truth was, I couldn't care less. All I cared about was that I got to make this woman mine for the rest of our lives.

# *Epilogue*

*Three Months Later*

"**M**om, seriously, you have got to stop crying," I pleaded as she stood behind me fiddling with the back of my dress for the hundredth time.

"You just wait, baby girl," she warned, wiping at her eyes. "When you're in my position, about to watch your baby get married... well, you just wait," she huffed through tears.

Her gentle warning was met with soft smiles from Jill, Olivia, Grace, Emmie, and Ginnie, who had all helped me get ready. Grace and Ginnie had worked my hair into a beautiful, elegant yet unique updo with a single braid interwoven in my dark strands. Grace had done my makeup, and as I stood looking in the mirror, I could barely believe the gorgeous woman that stared back was me.

The dress itself was relatively simple with a belted waist and plunging neckline. The deep slit that showed off lots of leg was where it stood out. Liv had fought like hell to get me to wear it. And now looking at myself, I was glad, as usual, that I'd listened to her.

After everything that had happened with Jared, Max and I didn't want to wait long to get married. Instead, we'd thrown ourselves into creating an outdoor oasis in the backyard. We'd cut down trees, cleared brush, and landscaped it into a perfect setting for our wedding.

It felt right to both of us to get married at home.

"The guys are having trouble keeping Max out of here," Ginnie shared with a grin as she looked at her phone, no doubt texting with X.

"Well he's just gonna have to wait," I replied. It was important to me that he didn't see me before the ceremony. Less so because of the superstition and more because I wasn't sure what he'd think of the dress.

"Won't be long now." My mom smiled through a sheen of tears.

Jill wrapped a supportive arm around her as they both looked at me through tears. When she approached, cupping my face in her hands, I had to bite back my own emotion.

"You make my son so happy," she murmured. "Thank you, Wren."

"He makes me happy too." I barely managed to speak around the lump in my throat.

"Now, you're marrying a Jackson man, I have a bit of advice that you probably don't need, but you're going to get it anyway."

I nodded with a grin, knowing there was no stopping her even if I wanted to.

"Our men, they're stubborn as hell, but you and I, we're cut from the same cloth. We're just as stubborn and usually right, am I right?" She winked. At my nod, she continued. "Let him win some, honey, especially when it comes to your safety. Let him be overprotective when he needs to be. Let him brood if he wants to, but force him to talk when you know he needs to. Let him be himself, but push him in the only way someone who truly loves him can." Tears were sliding down both our cheeks as she continued. "Let him eat all the muffins—I left you his favorite recipe." She smiled. "But most of all, just love the hell out of each other."

"We will," I promised.

"Let's get married." Her words were met by whoops of excitement from the women I'd loved for as long as I could remember.

A knock at the door had me biting back tears all over again because I knew it was my pop coming to get me. When he stepped inside, I watched him visibly swallow.

"You look beautiful," he told me hoarsely, opening his arm for me to press into his side.

"Thanks, Pop."

"You'll always be my baby, you know that?" he murmured, kissing the side of my head.

"I know," I agreed as Mom led the girls outside to find their seats. We weren't doing a formal ceremony, no bridesmaids or groomsmen. Our only wedding party member was Rosie, who would hopefully cooperate and bring us the rings.

Pop took my hand, and together we walked down the hallway and toward the patio doors that would lead me to my man. Nerves had my pulse racing as we stepped onto the deck and I caught sight of Max, looking incredible in black slacks and a vest, his muscular arms clasped in front of him as he waited.

The moment our eyes locked, my nerves disappeared and all I could think about was running toward him. I watched as Max's gaze slid slowly over my frame, devouring every inch. He shifted his stance as though impatient to get his hands on me.

That made two of us.

My pop pulled me back with a chuckle. "Soon enough, little bird."

The walk through our friends and family was a blur as I kept my eyes glued to Max. Finally, he was a breath away and my pop was placing my hand in his. He clapped Max on the shoulder. "Take care of her."

Max looked at him with an earnest nod. "With everything I am."

Cole cleared his throat, clearly ready to begin. We'd asked him to officiate our ceremony, wanting someone close to us, and Cole could command a room, there was that added bonus.

With Max's strong hands engulfing mine, my dream since childhood came true as I became his and he became mine.

I didn't even care when Rosie went rogue, and instead of running toward us, she took off toward the house with a squeal.

The sight of Gunner and Cash trying to grab her, swearing the entire time, made it well worth it. When X bellowed, "Grab the ham!" I thought I was going to lose it.

"You're finally mine," Max growled as he pulled me close for our first dance. The ceremony was over and our friends and family stood milling about, drinking and talking, the sound of joy booming off the trees that encircled our land.

"I've been yours," I reminded him with a smile.

He tweaked the rings on my left hand. "Now there's no doubt."

"No doubt," I assured him.

"This dress...." He trailed off. "Glad I didn't see it before—probably wouldn't have let you wear it, and you look hotter than hell," he admitted. "Those damn legs of yours." He shook his head as though to clear it.

I smiled. I knew my man too well.

He looked at something over my shoulder before turning back to me. "Gonna have you dance with your pop, baby," he murmured, dipping to kiss my lips gently. "This isn't easy for him, even if he's happy."

"No," I agreed, falling a little more in love with my man in that moment.

"I'll be right behind you."

I got to have this man at my back for the rest of my life, and I got to have his. It had been a wild ride to get here, but it was worth every misstep and every bump because it had led me here, to him.

Where I'd stay for the rest of my life.

~The End~

Thank you so much for reading!
Please consider leaving a review.

I'd love to connect with you!
*www.facebook.com/obrienbooks*
*Instagram: meganobrienbooks*
*Website: meganobrienbooks.com*

Made in United States
Orlando, FL
13 June 2022

18764780R00130